PATOUCHAS

PATOUCHAS

Ioannis Kondylakis

EFSTATHIADIS GROUP

EFSTATHIADIS GROUP S.A.
14, Valtetsiou Str.
106 80 Athens
Tel: (01) 5154650, 6450113
Fax: (01) 5154657
GREECE

ISBN 960 226 564 7

© **Efstathiadis Group S.A. 1999**

Cover design J. P. Mitrakas

Printed and bound in Greece

Contents

Page

Introduction 7

Chapter 1 19

Chapter 2 28

Chapter 3 47

Chapter 4 61

Chapter 5 71

Chapter 6 78

Chapter 7 129

Chapter 8 144

Chapter 9 158

Footnotes 166

Introduction

In the last quarter of the 19th century, Ioannis Kondylakis (1861-1920), and his fellow writers -- Alexandros Papadiamantis (1851-1911), Alexandros Moraitidis (1851-1929) and Andreas Karkavitsas (1866-1922) -- constituted what has been called the New School of Athens. The main objective of this group was ethography, recording for posterity traditional Greek life, which under the influence of the new Greek state and contact with Western Europe, was beginning to change. To describe the customs of rural, traditional Greece, these writers used several literary forms, pre-eminently the short story.

Papadiamantis, one of the leading lights of the movement, mastered the short story and brought it to maturity as a Greek form. He is best known for his analysis of the human psyche, especially in his novel, *The Murderess,* in which he explores the soul of a village woman who, in reaction to the oppressive life of the village, turns to violence and begins murdering female children. Moraitidis preoccupied himself with themes similar to those of Papadiamantis, except that the former was given more to the "painting of life than analyzing it."[1] Karkavitsas' devotion to *demotike,* the spoken language, was a major contribution to the development of modern Greek literature. The construction of his stories served as prototypes for many writers of his time. One of his best works, *The Beggar,* vividly portrays the misery of superstitious village life in mainland Greece.

These early authors made Greek prose a more supple and suitable vehicle for a variety of literary endeavors. Still, a problem which these writers faced at this time was that of language -- a peculiarly Greek problem which has troubled Greek life and letters for the past two centuries.

Even before the birth of the new Greek state, an important linguistic battle was joined, with consequences affecting present day Greece. After four hundred years of Turkish rule, under which, although schools had vanished from Greece, "semi-educated monks and priests taught young Greeks their language and their historical and religious inheritance," (Decavalles, p. 81), the Greek language had changed in many ways. Greek, as a language of the arts, of government, philosophy and science had atrophied; it lacked educated writers and an adequate vocabulary to express contemporary thought properly. Worst of all, according to some, it had absorbed an enormous number of loan words from Turkish, Italian and other European languages. Naturally, the question arose as to how Greek could best be restored to its former power and resiliency. From this lively debate over the future of the Greek language, two main positions emerged. One party, led by Yiannis Psycharis (1854-1929) -- who expounded and exemplified his theory about language in *My Journey,* published in 1898 -- argued that the language spoken by the majority of the people, the popular language, should be the basis of a national tongue. Others led by Adamantios Korais, held that a language purged of loan words and closer to ancient Greek *(katharevousa)* was a more dignified solution. The latter position carried the day, and except for poetry, *katharevousa* became the official language after 1821.

Demotike, however, had the long-term advantage of being a living language, the actual speech of the Greek people. And so, although influenced by *katharevousa,* it gained strength and slowly displaced the learned and artificial language from all of its strongholds -- the last being government documents and the classes and examinations at the University of Athens in 1975-1976.

A brief sketch of the political history of Crete might also be helpful to explain the use of some words in *Patouchas* and also the patriotic feelings of the Cretans during this same time. Though Crete was prominent among Greek states in the days of Homer, she played little significant role in historical antiquity. After the decline of the ancient Greek states, Crete was occupied successively by the Romans, the Byzantines, the Saracens, and the Venetians.

The occupation by the Venetians in 1204 has often been referred to as *Frankokratia.* From that period onwards, all westerners, their languages, dress, religion and customs were called *Frankish.* The words *Franks* and *Frankish,* as they are used in *Patouchas,* refer to virtually any things or persons who are considered foreign by the villagers. During the Frankokratia Italian words were incorporated in the Greek vocabulary, one of these being *Koubaros* which, in both the Italian and Greek languages, refers to a god-father and is also used as a term of familiarity and friendship.

In 1669 Crete became a part of the Ottoman Empire and, even though mainland Greece gained her independence around 1827, Turkish soldiers were not removed from Crete until 1898; not until 1912 was it finally restored to Greece. Thus, Kondylakis' novel has a nationalistic purpose as well as an ethographic one: to heighten the tension between Greeks and Turks and to keep the question of Crete in the foreground of the mainlanders' minds.

Ioannis Kondylakis was born in 1861 in Viannos, studied philosophy in Chania and taught in Modi, all on Crete. He was best known for, and is considered the father of the *chronographema,* a "short semi-journalistic, semi-literary article" (Decavalles, p. 81). He began to write these articles in the summer of 1889 for the newspapers *Asty, Ephemeris* and *Skrip* in Athens. His most serious work in the *chronographema* was done for the newspaper *Embros* in 1896. During this period, Kondylakis developed a liveliness and ironic humor evident throughout his later work. Over a period of thirty years Kondylakis wrote almost six thousand articles. By comparison, his purely literary work is quite limited. Written while he was working for the newspapers, the short story "When I Was a Teacher," and the novels *First Love* and *Patouchas,* are the best examples of his literary talent. It is generally agreed that *Patouchas* is the best of them. Alkis Thrylos goes so far as to say that *Patouchas* was, for its author, "the beginning and the end to Kondylakis' career."[2]

Kondylakis wrote at a time when the demoticists were attempting to claim prose literature as their domain. Although he uses *katharevousa* for the descriptive and narrative passages, Kondylakis makes certain concessions to demotic in that his language is simple and without the pedantic affectations of some of his predecessors. In addition, his dialogue reproduces the actual speech of Cretan villagers. Thus, *Patouchas,* containing both languages, embodies the language problem in a somewhat hybrid way, though in this work Kondylakis treats the problem comfortably if not always successfully. He apparently believed that the descriptive and narrative passages should be given an elevated tone, and he handled ironic and tragicomic elements more pointedly by use of *katharevousa* rather than *demotike.* Dialogue, on the other hand, had to sound real and as close to the spoken language as possible; therefore, it was necessary to employ the Cretan dialect for speech. While the Cretan dialect is not strictly *demotike,* the concept behind its use in *Patouchas* is basically the same: it, too, is the language of the people. Though it is a bold attempt, this mixture of *katharevousa* with Cretan dialect creates a tension which can be best felt by comparing *Patouchas* with *First Love,* a short novel published before *Patouchas,* and written wholly in *demotike.* The language in this novel is quite lyrical and notably superior to the hybrid mixture in

Patouchas, which by comparison experiments with language rather than using language to fit content or theme. Unfortunately, Kondylakis·did not live long enough to give full expression to his obvious ability in the popular language for he died in 1920.

Since Kondylakis, along with his contemporaries, considered the past "a priceless inheritance whose understanding was indispensable for Greece as she faced her national and social·problems," (Decavalles, p. 80), he consciously wrote about these problems in his work. *Patouchas,* "When I Was a Teacher" and other short stories, foresee prophetically the coming independence of his homeland. Kondylakis often digresses on the hatred between Greeks and Turks, because he feels compelled to let the reader know how the Greeks in remote villages felt about their oppressors the Turks, and how they too had done their part for the independence of Crete and its union with Greece.

André Andréadès has said that "Condylakis ne s'inspirait de personne, il racontait tout bonnement à ses amis d'Athènes ce qu'il avait vu dans son île natale."[3] In *Patouchas* Kondylakis introduces the reader to the life and mores of Cretan villages and their inhabitants in a clever and engaging manner. He does this by placing Manolis, the untutored and near-savage shepherd in the midst of the highly organized social structure of a traditional village. The conflict between the two, as the shepherd adapts to the village, and *vice versa,* makes the rules of village society clear, as well as giving full expression to the instinctive impulses of man which they are meant to curb. The *rites de passages* as expressed in specific events and situations in the novel, are the result of a well-organized plot and careful attention to detail in the process of showing the hero's initiation into manhood.

As soon as Saitonicolis, Manolis' father, gets a chance, he takes his son for a tour in the village. One important action, which at first sight might look to be a habitual instead of an initiating experience for Manolis, is Saitonicolis' introduction of his son into Smyrnios' cafe where they sit down and drink a demi-tasse of Greek coffee. He is introduced to the society of men: going to cafes, drinking coffee and discussing matters of importance to the village and its inhabitants, as well as ethnic and more universal questions. It is essential for Manolis to learn how to act like the rest of the men of the village.

Another similar event, which entails the forging of social links, is the baptism. What is important in Manolis' involvement here is the role of the *koubaros.* In becoming the baby's god-father Manolis forges important links beyond those of the extended family unit. Apart from the close relationship which will henceforth exist between Manolis' and Moustovasilis' families, Manolis will be responsible for his god-daughter's spiritual and physical welfare, since he is considered her spiritual father. He will also have a say when the time comes for his god-child's marriage. On the other hand, Manolis will be able to depend on Moustovasilis' support as he adapts to village life, and as he faces other problems in later life.

His father's terms (as well as those of the community), before he is allowed to get married, are to build a two-story house. It is expected that the parents of the bride or of the groom provide a home for the newly married couple. Traditionally, the home is considered to be part of the bride's dowry. However, Saitonicolis insists that his son build a two-story house. Manolis considers a second-story superfluous, but his father refuses to make concessions because the community expects him to build a house reflective of his wealth. Since Saitonicolis is considered a well-to-do villager, he has to build a large house for his son so his reputation will not be at stake. Of course, there is also the justification that Manolis needs the extra time to become further socialized.

Manolis' pre-engagement, to Pighi is important for several reasons. Two young people about to be married must first go through three stages. The pre-engagement entails giving one's word or *logos,* meaning that the parents of each of the young people agree that their children will become engaged and then married. Usually the *logos* is given when much preparation has to be done before the marriage can take place but the families want the community to know that the young people are spoken for. During this period the young people do not have the right to be alone together. The *logos* is more easily broken than an engagement and, in case it is broken the girl does not run so much risk of being considered unmarriageable. Engagement is a ceremony in itself, during which the priest blesses the couple, puts the golden bands on their fingers as a symbol of their impending union. During this period the two young people are allowed to be seen together by the rest of the community, since the engagement means they are going to be married fairly soon. This explains Thomas' and Stratis' strict treatment of Manolis when the latter insists on seeing Pighi alone. The families had only promised them to one another, the father and son are justified in the eyes of the rest of the community.

Saitonicolis' insistence that Manolis is not yet ready for marriage involves not only being true to the custom of the above-mentioned arrangement and the delay of sexual gratification, but something much more important which also makes Saitonicolis a unique character. Manolis himself is the one who must decide when and if he will marry on the basis of his own understanding of what life in the adult world involves. Even though his experiences during the two years he lives in the village contribute to Manolis' gaining such understanding, what finally pushes him into maturity is the experience with the widow, Zervoudhena. This experience is also an initiation into the occasionally terrifying world of the sexes. Zervoudhena is not treated as sympathetically by Kondylakis as, for example, Kazantzakis treats the widow in *Zorba the Greek.* Kazantzakis shows the cruelty of the villagers in order to criticize the oppressive demands of social ritual. In *Patouchas* Kondylakis shows that the treatment of the widow by the villagers is somehow natural since widows traditionally are not supposed to remarry. It is the custom and the value system of the village. They all have to abide by it.

Kondylakis seems to be telling us that behavior which is inappropriate to the norms of that or any traditional village in Crete can only hurt the person who so deviates.

Unlike Kazantzakis, or even Papadiamantis, who both attacked what they considered the unjust treatment of women, Kondylakis is satisfied to describe things as they are. If he is to live comfortably and happily among village people, Manolis must do his best to conform. He will probably never be entirely domesticated, but he must learn to live without grave friction among men.

Another but not insignificant initiation experience is the restraint of physical passion or aggression and its replacement with wit. For more than half of the story Manolis is presented as impulsive and violent. Whenever he is insulted or angered, he reacts with physical violence, as for example, in his attacks on Tereres, the unrestrained expression of his passion for Pighi, the incident with Marghi's donkey and his attempt to kill Smyrnios. At the dance, however, we see a different and socialized Manolis. When Tereres makes fun of Manolis because he sings the same *mattinadas* over and over, Manolis instantly feels the impulse to strike Tereres, but instead he decides to engage in a verbal contest by improvising a witty *mattinada,* making fun of Tereres' threat to bind him. Kondylakis could not have found a better way to show us that Manolis is finally beginning to learn how to live among the villagers and at the same time be accepted by them.

A final observation may be made concerning the hero's instincts in contrast to the cruelty of village life. It is clear that Manolis leaves the village to become a shepherd in the mountains not merely because he wants to get away from the monk, the schoolteacher, and letters but because he is a natural, instinctual being who flees the demand of civilization that he postpone gratification of his desires and become its servant first. He feels that since he can be a perfect shepherd who recognizes all his sheep and goats individually, why should he bother with school? But the libidinal impulse which leads him away from the village, leads him back to it. When Manolis sees the billy-goat surrounded by his harem of nanny-goats, he realizes that the force which has of late been making him behave strangely, is somehow connected to the sexual behavior of all living beings. And that quite simply is why Manolis comes to live in the village for good. He has not changed in any way. He is still acting for the immediate satisfaction of his desires. Of course, the villagers react according to their socially acceptable values and, even though the community to which Patouchas has to adapt, is itself changing (as shown in the examples of Smyrnios, who has travelled abroad, and of Marghi, who brings a new fashion and a new name from the city to the village), Kondylakis' hero still wants socializing to a considerable extent.

Most important, Kondylakis makes sure the reader understands that Manolis would be in a very difficult situation, if not an impossible one, if he did not have his father to protect him against the reaction of the villagers. The kind of suffering Manolis might have to suffer is suggested by the working-out of a sub-plot, in Chapter II, concerning the dog's experience. Both Three-Eyes, Manolis' dog, and Manolis himself are protected from their enemies by the intervention of the people closest to them. Just as Manolis is protected by his father, the dog is protected by Manolis. To remain in the village, both must learn to adapt to the expectations of its inhabitants before they can act alone and with confidence. Three-Eyes' experiences parallel his master's except that they are more direct and more physically painful. The conversation Manolis has with his dog at the end of Chapter II draws a faint line between humans and animals. Manolis says to his dog: "If you were Manolis, you would like it; but you are only a dog, poor fellow!" This is a comment on animal instincts, both in animals and in humans, which exist just below the facade of human civility. The battle of the dogs for territory also reflects, at the same time, the ever-present struggle between Greeks and Turks.

Saitonicolis' protection of his son exposes us to the traditional family structure of 19th century Greece. There is usually the stern father who will have his way in all family matters, the solicitous mother who is more indulgent and often acts as an intermediary between her children and her husband, and finally there is the supportive extended family, to which Manolis often resorts to complain and for refuge. We also see how Saitonicolina, Manolis' mother, always tries to mediate between them when Saitonicolis and his son are antagonistic to each other. Traditional parents are willing to sacrifice themselves for their children in order to preserve the good name of the family. But when a child goes completely astray, as Manolis does by stubbornly running after Zervoudhena's daughter, then their responsibility to the community and respect for its customs prevails over parental love. This is what in fact happens when, outside the church, the elders and other men of the village gather to decide what kind of action to take to restrain and socialize Manolis. Saitonicolis, who so far had been much concerned about his son's behavior, now lets the elders decide to do whatever they want to with Manolis.

What finally changes the attitude of all the villagers, even that of Spyridolenia, the village gossip, is Manolis' brave attack on one of the young Turkish *agas* who went to the dance to cause trouble. Manolis' action is just as impulsive as the rest of his previous behavior, but the villagers approve of it because of their hatred for the Turks. Indirectly, Manolis learns that before he can get married or be accepted in the community he has to channel his behavior into socially acceptable ways. Even violent behavior is acceptable if it is directed at the enemies of the community such as the Turks and their Albanian police.

An important characteristic of traditional Greek society is the role of honor and shame. The men protect a family's honor, while the duty of the women is to avoid shaming it. In *Patouchas* Kondylakis shows us how feverishly the parents and brothers of unmarried young women fight to keep their family's honor. Thomas and Stratis justifiably go to extremes to keep their family's reputation intact. Stratis goes as far as to shoot Manolis when the former finds the latter trying to abduct Pighi. Marghi's mother, even while encouraging Manolis' persistence, makes sure that the community has the impression that it is he who is imposing his attention on her daughter. Stratis would have been supported by the rest of the community had he killed Manolis. Honor and shame play a deadly serious role in traditional society. They can lead to murder and engender feuds which lead to the eradication of entire families. In the *Sun of Death,* Pandelis Prevelakis gives the dark side of this kind of Cretan feuding, which leads to countless reprisals. In *Zorba the Greek,* the widow's death ransoms the honor of the young man who drowns himself. In *Patouchas* Kondylakis softens with comedy what in real life could have terrible consequences. Manolis only suffers the secret shame of having his backside filled with buckshot. As for Marghi, she, too, stops going out altogether to avoid the risk of being abducted by Manolis. Kondylakis does not show the effects of shame on a family, but he does show us how far people will go to avoid it. In real life if a girl, especially, a poor one such as Pighi, were put to shame, it is almost certain that she would never marry. This is why Thomas says to Saitonicolis that his family's honor is all that he has left in the world and he cannot afford to lose it. Even Spyridolenia decides to undo what she has wrought by appealing for public support when she realizes that Marghi's chances for marriage are being endangered by Manolis' antics. Kondylakis avoids the serious side of his hero's misdeeds while depending on our awareness of their possible implications to heighten their comic effect.

By the time Manolis' father takes his son's misconduct seriously, it is almost too late. It is from here onwards that Kondylakis slides from the purely comic to the tragi-comic. Two situations with tragi-comic undertones are the discussion among the elders about what to do in the face of Manolis' disturbing behavior, and the last encounter of Manolis with the widow. In both cases Manolis escapes any permanent personal damage. The fight with the Turks permits him to save face with the village and the darkness of the night saves him from being shamed by his association with the widow. Decavalles describes Kondylakis' special strengths as a writer when he says of him: "In the midst of tragedy his brilliant humor comes to alleviate pain and avert catastrophe. His work is full of antitheses and surprise and reflects the tragicomic reality of life" (Decavalles, p. 81).

One of Kondylakis' strongest points is his ability to inspire even his most peripheral characters with life and unique personalities as he does with Barbarezos, an idler and a moocher, Astronomos, the pseudo-scientist and dreamer, and Sykologos the builder who is proud of his singing even though he has a terrible voice. The uniqueness of Saitonicolis' character lies in his ability to look at the funny side of things while he uses his sense of humor to temper them. If it were not for the beautiful off-color anecdotes which he often improvises to teach Manolis a lesson, his son might not have been able to support the pressures of socialization. Finally, there are Spyridolenia, the village gossip, who is a real character because she is so typically a traditional gossip, and Smyrnios, who uses personal means to reach a patriotic end.

Another stylistic device the author uses for serious comic purposes is the naming of his characters. The name Saitonicolis comes from the word *saita* which means arrow or shuttle, and from the Christian name Nicolis. Both an arrow and a shuttle imply the straightforwardness which characterizes Saitonicolis. The name of his wife, Reginia, comes from the Greek word for peace, *irene*. Short for Irene is Renio and people in Greek villages ended up saying Reginio, instead of Renio, because it is more comfortable to pronounce. However, also note the similarity between Reginio and the Italian female name, Regina, which means queen. Reginia often act as the peacemaker between her son and her husband or between the former and Pighi. Tereres' name means to twitter like a bird. It refers to a sort of shrill, meaningless sound, but it does suggest his risible chanting in church as well as his power to cast spells by magic incantation. The name suggests the author's contempt for both abilities. Astronomos suggests a star-gazer and by extension, one with his head in the clouds. When one morning several of the villagers discuss the heavy fog that has appeared, Astronomos predicts that a plague or a sickness will come to the village -- it never does. He philosophizes instead of cultivating the land. When he predicts a date when the liberation of Constantinople should take place, the villagers believe him because they want it badly to happen, not because there is any proof that Astronomos' predictions will come true. Barbarezos is a name given to a Moslem coming from the Barbary Coast. It is a Greek village way of referring to North Africa, and in this particular context he is called Barbarezos because he is suspected of being an informer to the Moslem Turks, and therefore is considered a foreigner or an outsider. Zervoudhena's name means to be left-handed and that suggests her clumsiness at expressing her desires to Manolis and her *gaucheness* in fostering the delusions of her daughter. Her nickname, Gadfly, comes from her habits as a gadfly, annoying and sticking to Manolis until she goes mad. Finally, Manolis' nickname, Patouchas, means that he has big feet but it also implies that he has big genitals taken from both modern and ancient meanings. We never doubt Manolis' masculinity but his fear of Tereres which almost gives him the reputation of a coward is a comic commentary on the masculinity of this youth. Of course in the end, Manolis proves that he is not a coward but also learns to control and channel his sexual instincts.

For the English reader, the various inflected endings of Greek names can be confusing. A name can be made more familiar and affectionate by adding suffixes. Thus, Manolis is also called Manolios, Pighi is also called Pighio; Marouli, Maroulio; Reginia, Reginio; Lenia, Lenio and so on. In other cases, names are abbreviated. Saitonicolis becomes Nicolis or Nicolios. A daughter may be called by the name of one of her parents with the suffix-*poula*. So Pighi is also called Thomopoula since her father is Thomas, and Marghi is called Zervodhopoula. A wife may also be called by the name of her husband with a varying suffix added to it. For example Saitonicolis' wife is at times called Saitonicolina.

Although Kondylakis occasionally permits himself to digress from the subject at hand, especially to describe the enmity between Greeks and Turks, he presents a tightly woven story. For example, Kondylakis often repeats certain incidents in different contexts, both for comic effect and to make us aware of how Manolis is adapting to civilized life. In the second chapter, when Saitonicolis takes his son for a tour of the village, he asks Pighi to throw them a sprig of basil. Later on in the novel, Manolis, imitating his father, asks Marghi for a sprig of basil at one of his visits outside her house. Instead of basil, he gets a soaking. Even so, this is evidence that Manolis becomes socialized by identifying himself with his father and imitating his behavior.

Another instance of how closely linked the various parts of *Patouchas* are, is the scene in which Pighi stands at her doorstep with the last rays of the afternoon sun falling upon her. The first time we see Pighi in such a pose occurs when Manolis falls in love with her, and so his reaction to seeing her thus is one of overflowing affection. After Manolis deserts Pighi and is in hot pursuit of Marghi, he happens to pass by Pighi's house and the scene is repeated. This time, however, the scene is one of sadness which, in contrast to the previous scene, underscores Pighi's suffering.

While the above discussion centers on the stylistic means Kondylakis uses to describe the *rites de passage* of a young man in a traditional Greek setting, he further contributes to the sense of time and place with a liberal sprinkling of proverbs, snatches of folksongs and popular poetry throughout the book. Folk sayings and Saitonicolis' anecdotes are ritualistic means of showing how to face problems of everyday life. They are a means of giving direct advice to younger people, as Saitonicolis does to Manolis, and of consoling persons in distress. By including these folksayings, Kondylakis shows the close ties the Greek people have to their traditions and also to emphasize the comic elements in the story. Even Manolis cannot keep from smiling at his father's anecdotes which allude to his personal situation, or to the builders' scandalous song about the young man who is in love with Aunt Irene.

Kondylakis' characters have been compared by Andréadès to those of Dickens and Daudet. The basis of this comparison lies in the true, vital and realistic secondary characters. Kondylakis' characters are all as vividly portrayed and interesting in their own unique way as Dicken's Sikes or Nancy and even Chaucer's Wife of Bath and the Pardoner. Can we forget Stratis, the passionate hunter and perfectly traditional brother who will do anything to preserve his sister's honor? Or Thomas, the strict father and lonely widower? They all represent aspects of the tight structure of a culture, and so each one plays a significant role.

With a few words or an incident Kondylakis introduces us to characters we seem to have known forever. One can say that even now, in modern Greece, it is possible to see the characters found in *Patouchas* in the Greek countryside. However, despite the local color, there is more than an exotic quaintness which enlivens Kondylakis' novel in our minds because, beneath it all, the characters and the situations in which they find themselves have a universality which makes them impinge on our own experience. From his celebration of libidinal instincts to the reminders of the mixture of noble, base, conscious and unconscious motivations behind human behavior, Kondylakis speaks to an audience far from his native Crete in time and place.

18

1. Ho Patouchas: The Bigfooted Greek

The event of the day in the village was the arrival of Saitonicolis son, almost unknown until he suddenly appeared one Sunday in 1863, an eighteen year-old of extraordinary proportions, a mountain of a man as tall as the sky. Damn Saitonicolis, what a son he has bred! Just look at that size, look at those shoulders. Can you imagine what he will look like when he enters adulthood? He was only a child yesterday. How did he manage all of a sudden to spurt into such a gigantic man?

Naturally he had not been in a city. It was evident a mile away. After the first impression, all those who loved gossiping began to find different marks of imperfection in the young man, and mocking laughter succeeded their admiration. It was said, for instance, that having lived far from people (being a shepherd in the mountains since he was a little boy), he had become an animal among animals except that he didn't butt. He did not even know how to talk clearly and if he happened to find himself among people, he would lose control like a wild goat looking for a way to escape.

Spyridolenia, the most celebrated gossip of the village and because of this, the most fear-inspiring, was always ready, if one stumbled, to compose a witty and mocking little poem about him. When she saw Saitonicolis' son, she pretended to be frightened by him, "Mother!" Then she laughed with her drawn out, dry laugh, and leaning towards the woman sitting next to her, whispered the following improvised epigram:

> Here comes he with the huge hands and cheeks
> With the monstrous stature and gigantic feet.

This couplet with which Spyridolenia drew, as if by a single pen-stroke, the young man's caricature, was transmitted from ear to ear, accompanied by chuckling laughter. It also produced a frivolous atmosphere in the circle of women seated under the plane-tree, dressed in their Sunday clothes and watching those coming from the cross-roads. One of the women fell into spasmodic, unquenchable laughter holding one hand over her breasts, while with the other, she tapped Lenia's shoulder and said: "Oh my God, I'm going to burst with laughter. I hope it brings me luck!"

While they watched the young man walking in the distance with long arms hanging like useless, whimsical appendages, with long legs to which the agitation of that head, that perfect colossus, was transmitted, stumbling over stones like a blindman, as though he were confused by a fear of people, the humor of the epigrammatic picture appeared more and more fitting and the laughter continued.

Within a few hours the couplet had made a complete tour of the village accompanied by a mocking nickname. Inspired by his broad feet, the most outstanding characteristic of this remarkable youth, Spyridolenia to add the finishing touch named him "Patouchas."

Manolis, now renamed Patouchas, had manifested from an early age such a love for the shepherd's life that it was with great difficulty his father managed to detach him from the sheep in order to hand him over to the schoolteacher, a monk who had recently started a school where he gave more spankings than lessons. The monk taught *koine,* the so-called ecclesiastical tongue, to prepare readers who could chant in church and who carried in their belts, as a symbol of their worthiness, the long, brass stylus. But within a period of fifteen days, Manolis did not manage to learn anything more than the phrase, "Holy Cross preserve us," which was held to be more important than the alphabet. The teacher, having exhausted all lesser punitive measures on him and having broken over his back dozens of switches, decided to try the famous and dreadful *falanga.*[4] Manolis, who had a fearful idea of this pedagogical torture, showed desperate resistance. The monk, however, being helped by the better students, managed to seize his naked legs and submit them to the *falanga,* giving the soles of his feet forty strokes less one.

The child, with bleeding feet, swore never to return to that hell again. But his father also swore "to make a human out of him;" he did not want his son to remain an unsculpted block of wood and the next day he forcibly led the imploring and crying Manolis to school and gave the teacher the awesome order: "Preserve only the bones, teacher." The teacher conscientiously followed the father's request, but Manolis, the most directly concerned, did not share his father's opinion. And one day, flinging a sheet of paper hooked on a reed at the teacher, he turned to flight. Instead of going to the paternal hearth, whence he would again be led the following day to the terrible monk, he turned in the direction of the mountains and within a few hours he reached his father's sheep-fold.

When he arrived there, amid the familiar mountains, the familiar trees and the familiar animals, his only true acquaintances and friends, he was overcome by the emotion and joy of the person who returns to his native land which he had never hoped to see again. And he would have danced like a mad man if his joy had not been lessened by the fear that his father would come to take him back to school. This insistence seemed to him completely unreasonable. What did he want letters for when he was so well off as he was, so contented? Whatever he desired in order to be happy, he had; he wanted to be a shepherd and he was a shepherd. Why did they tear him away from happiness and condemn him to sit still for hours, beneath the threat of a mean man's fierce look within four walls? To learn letters? What would he do with letters? He was still going to become a shepherd and no one he knew among the shepherds was literate. Moreover, he had come to the conviction that it was impossible for him to learn letters. He was already frightened of them when the terror which the teacher inspired provoked such agitation in him that his memory and his tongue were paralyzed as one. He received countless slaps in order to become accustomed to calling "A", *alpha;* and when he did learn one of the letters of the alphabet he would forget the preceding one; and if the teacher approached him, he would forget everything or he would confuse one thing with the other.

And yet, he who couldn't manage to learn the twenty-four letters of the alphabet, knew all his father's sheep and goats separately, and they were no small number. How could it be that as a shepherd he was so sharp, and in school so disconcerted that he was indistinguishable from the wooden bench beneath him? Could the other children whistle as he did, throw a stone as far in the manner of a shepherd? Did anyone know the marks on the goats and sheep as he did? Even now, if they'd let him, he was capable of milking and even of cheese-making.

When he returned to his mountains, it was as though a dark fog had departed from his mind and a weight which had bound the limbs of his body lifted. It seemed to him that he was free just like the birds flying around him.

Upon seeing his parents and his brothers again, he never felt the joy which he felt upon seeing the familiar places, the sheep and the goats, who watched him with a look of pleasant surprise as if to say: "Welcome! What have you been up to so long?" And with a general jangling of bells they seemed to celebrate his return. His true family was those guileless animals and the still more innocent trees, and the rocks, and the wild flowers which, one could say, addressed to him, a friendly greeting as they swayed on the precipices. Everything, living and inanimate, smiled at him with tenderness which he possibly saw only on the maternal visage. Even the crows, cawing from high up above, seemed friends to him.

The sheep dogs had hurried to meet him, delirious with joy. When they met, Manolis rolled in the grass with them, returning their endearments like a dog, and speaking to them as though they were people:

"You thought that I'd never come back to the mountains, huh? I was afraid of it too. Ah, fellas, it's bad in the village, especially when they put you in school. Do you have any idea what school is? It's a place where all the lads go every day and there there's a monk, whom they call teacher, and he spanks them."

From an understandable delicateness, Saitonicolis's son avoided relating to his friends the humiliating incident of the *falanga*. He expressed to them only his irritation with the monk and said that, if they met him some day, they would certainly straighten him out, quite well, with their teeth.

As Manolis had foreseen, his father came to the sheepfold for the purpose of bringing him back to school either through persuasion or by way of force. He came up several times, but his effort was in vain. Whenever Manolis saw him he would flee like a wild animal and shout, crying:

"I don't want to go to school! I don't want to!"

He threatened that, if his father insisted, he would hurl himself to his death in the nearby ravine.

So sincere was his voice and so decisive his regard, that Saitonicolis feared that, if he attempted to use force, his son would execute his threat. Finally, despairing, he left him to the wrath of God. "My son, I want you to have a thousand sheep, but if you don't want that, not even a tail. And we will see who will regret it."

In his solitude, in the quiet of the mountains and of the winter quarters, it was not long before Manolis became totally wild. The fear which was inspired in him by the teacher was transformed into an all encompassing fear of people. He feared with the terror of a wild animal and, like one, upon seeing a person, was prepared to turn to flight and hide. The only people he did not fear were his comrades, shepherds and cheesemakers, half-savage as he was. Yet, while they would go down to the village from time to time, in order to attend church and to take communion, Manolis never felt such a need. Of religion he retained a rudimentary and vague idea. He was dimly aware of things concerning Heaven and Hell; he knew the "Lord's Prayer" and "Christ is Risen," lamentably distorted, however. His prayers then consisted mainly of making the sign of the cross and kneeling. When there was thunder and lightning, he would make the sign of the cross and, terrified, whisper: "Remember me, Lord, remember me, Lord." In thunder he saw the threat of divine indignation, just as in the joy of blossoming and light-swathed nature he saw the smile of divine goodness. His God was a gigantic old man with a deep white beard and bushy eyebrows, residing in the spacious heavens, whence his wrathful gaze discharged the horrible lightning through the clouds.

His abandonment of his lessons did not distress his parents as much as his forgetting of his religious duties. A year and more had gone by since his flight and during this time, neither did he take communion nor did he attend the liturgy in church. His father had to spit blood before he could convince him to descend to the village solely for the purpose of taking communion. He made promises, he threatened him with damnation, he told him that his mother wept because she longed to see him, but Manolis remained unmoved; it was only when his father told him that, in insisting on not going to church and in not taking communion, he would become a Turk, for Turks neither go to church nor do they take communion, he began to think about it and finally consented.

He came down to the village at night and in the morning went to church, he gathered himself into a corner like a hare, which felt an eagle flying above, and having taken communion, he set out immediately for the mountains. Gradually, however, he became bolder and would descend two and three times a year in order to go to church. Nevertheless, he retained the nervous unease and the flashing eyes of a partially tamed animal.

His mother's efforts contributed to this gradual taming. While accompanying him to church, she taught him how to behave. When the liturgy was over, he had to stay in the churchyard and greet the villagers, and put his hand on his chest and bow his head: "Good day, your lordships." Next, he had to listen to the villagers talk and solve their differences before the elders, "So that he would gain experience." And, finally, when the priest came out, he approached, kissed his hand and left. Manolis followed his mother's advice for quite some time and, indeed, began to like church, especially when they distributed consecrated bread and boiled wheat.

But he still could not get accustomed to people, who did not begin to suspect his anthropophobia, because such phenomena were then, and perhaps still are, rare in the villages of Crete. One such day, after the liturgy, Vourgaris, a village prankster, approached him stealthily and suddenly with all his breath emitted a thundrous noise, "Pouf!" Manolis, agitated like a wild cat, jumped up and turned to flight, while the villagers laughed loudly and shouted after him as though at a fleeing hare pursued by dogs:

"Hey, you, catch him!"

After this comic mishap, he discontinued his relations with people for a long time. Whenever he came down for communion, he did not linger in the churchyard anymore, but departed immediately.

In his solitude his imagination personified everything and created a chimerical world in which he did not feel alone. In that world moreover, some of his fellow villagers were found. In the shapes and the profiles of the rocks he found resemblances to their physiognomies. Thus, in a big slab which stood opposite the sheepfold, he saw the countenance of one of their neighbors, Petroyianina. Another black rock, higher up, seemed just like Tzambotzas, the Arab, who went from door to door and begged. It used to be one of Manolis' pastimes to throw stones at him. Like Manolis, the children of the village threw stones at him too, but when he turned his black face and his teeth glittered, aahhhh! the children ran away. Then, he saw Father Dimitris in the huge, old oak tree and further up in the rock, a Turk with his turban. He knew this Turk, this Mavrobrahim. It was said that he had killed one of his uncles and so Manolis' father always struggled fiercely with him. And for this reason, Manolis, too, hated him and whenever he passed by him did not miss the opportunity to throw a few stones at him.

This was Patouchas' enemy. He hated him even more than he did the teacher. Everybody else, rocks, trees, flowers which smiled on the high stones, the springs which murmured among the branches and the clear pebbles, were his friends. However, his best friend was Theodoris. He was neither a rock nor a tree; he wasn't anything. He was only a hoarse voice which came from the depths of a narrow valley and whatever one shouted, he repeated as though mocking him. "Hey!" one would say to it; "hey!" he answered immediately. This was Theodoris, a little shepherd, who had the bad habit of stealing goats and sheep. And for this reason he had been petrified there in the gorge and was cursed to repeat every voice.

The older shepherds told this story to the younger ones, in order to prevent them from stealing animals; but they themselves believed the story so little that it did not dissuade them from stealing even more than Theodoris.

Manolis, passing by, always greeted the petrified shepherd: "Good-day, Theodoris." -- "Good-day, Theodoris," answered the voice. And Manolis would laugh at the foolishness or misfortune of the animal rustler.

"No, you silly fool!" he shouted at him.

"No, you silly fool," the ever incorrigible Theodoris would shout back.

And so Manolis never felt lonely and was always satisfied with his life.

But then a change occurred. In the first place, he grew up. His father gave him reason to notice this fact, when he went to the sheepfold once and, upon seeing him, exclaimed:

"Well, this lad has grown up. May he be preserved from the evil eye."

Grown up, he said? Then Manolis remembered that for quite some time he had been obliged to stoop like the older shepherds in order not to ram his head against the wooden lintel of the cheese-dairy. The truth is that the door of the cheese-dairy had no right to be called great; but just a short while ago it had been high for Manolis' height. He had occasion to make other comparisons, and now had no doubt that he was no longer a child. The thought that he was grown up gave him a sense of pride which he did not know how to express because it was impossible to imagine all of the consequences of such a transformation. However, the thought that he was approaching manhood and power, with a moustache and a beard, gave him powerful and deep emotions, from which it followed, specifically, that he would become completely free and master of himself.

When he passed by Theodoris' narrow valley, he announced to him the important event:

"Theodoris! See how I've grown up!"

But silly Theodoris, instead of congratulating him, repeated, as always, the identical phrase.

It is possible that Manolis could have noticed something else, characteristic of the change, but perhaps he missed it. His voice became deep and husky, like the sound of young cockerels on their way to becoming roosters.

But with the passing of the initial excitement and after he had become accustomed to the novelty, he began to lose the recent serenity of his life. A vague anxiety overcame him, as though he were missing something, which he did not know about and which it was impossible for him to divine. And during those moments he would come to rest as though petrified in abstraction with his eyes fixed upon the void, without seeing and without hearing. And in his heart dripped a melacholy, approximating nostalgia, with the difference that the nostalgia of the young shepherd did not have a particular direction. He longed for the unknown; and he was not conscious of what it was he longed for.

By contrast, at other times, an excessive joy overcame him, like a paroxysm of madness; and holding a branch, he leapt attempting to imitate the sound of a lyre with his mouth. Or, without reason, he chased the he-goats and nanny goats from an unrestrained necessity to run and jump and to conquer a passionate force, a seething juice of new life, which circulated in his veins and transmitted intoxicating fumes to his head. Many times the valleys echoed with his shouts, to which he tried to give the rhythm of song. But from among the songs that he had heard, his memory retained only one verse and he repeated it with the invariable prelude: "Ah! aman! aman!"

"Two wire bullets will I put in my gun . . . ."

But yet another change came into his soul. Specifically, he was no longer pleased with the life to which he had returned a few years back with so much joy. The chimerical world in which he had lived until now and which had been a complete life began to appear empty and false to him. Moments came when his thoughts longed passionately for another world, equally fantastic, but which shared characteristics with the village. It had, for example, a well where every evening girls would gather hurriedly with their water jugs as the church bell and two or three wooden gongs called them to vespers. That bell, of course, was at St. George's which had been hung from a wooden rod, next to the door. Now that he had grown up, he, too, could reach up to ring it. How he had admired and how jealous he had been, when he was in the village, of those who could reach up and ring the bell! Once his father lifted him up too and helped him hit the clapper. How delighted and how frightened he was at the same time when he heard the sound that he had made with his hand! He was then very little and because he kept asking to be lifted to ring the bell he was frightened into not asking again when he was told that there was an old woman whom he feared inside the bell and he believed it.

That world of his desires became a beautiful dream which he saw while awake amidst the apotheosis of a sunset, in the serenity of which the reverberation of the bell was hushed. In that symphony of colors and the rise and fall of the sound within the rosy haze, dawned moving and vague shadows which came gradually out of the dreamy obscurity, until, in the young man's ecstasy, there appeared in playful tangles, the forms of flesh-colored maidens whose glances and smiles were filled with sweet promises.

Seated on a high stone, before which his scattered goats and sheep grazed, Manolis remained plunged in the enchantment of his reverie for a long time, until the coarse bleating of a he-goat, prolonged by the echo of the ravines, brought him back to reality, and the beautiful apparitions departed and disappeared, like sparrows flying away. The young shepherd sighed; and turning about saw the he-goat shake his scanty mephistophelian beard over the edge of a high precipice and emit a new cry of triumph, "baaa!" His glance descended from the he-goat onto the nanny goats who with an effort at coquetry raised their foolish eyes towards the sultan. And a new sigh accompanied the thoughts of the young man. Why shouldn't he too be a he-goat?

2

You can imagine his parents' surprise when, one evening, they saw him arrive without any previous invitations or requests. His mother made the sign of the cross, praising God for enlightening him. Naturally, this event, for which one could not have hoped, was a miracle. However, Saitonicolis feared that something bad had happened, that thieves had entered the sheepfold and anxiously asked him why he had come down.

"I came to see you," Manolis answered simply.

But after he sat down in the darkest corner of the house, as was his custom, he said something amazing:

"I shall also stay in the village for two or three days. Am I going to live only in the mountains, like some wild creature?"

Indeed he said this with such determination in his voice, it was as though his parents had tried to prohibit his return to the village.

Saitonicolis exchanged a look of surprise and joy with his wife.

"Stay, my child, as long as you want," his mother said. "And if you want to stay for good, so much the better; it would be a pleasure for us."

"It was not we who wanted you to become a shepherd; you became one by yourself," Saitonicolis added, "and if you want to be with us, we want it a thousand times, my son."

The entire family celebrated that evening. All the relatives, aunts and uncles, and Manolis' older sister with her husband, came to greet the returned rebel; and joy radiated from each person's face, as if Saitonicolis' first born had died and was now risen from the dead. Nevertheless they avoided the customary endearments because they knew that kisses agitated him almost as much as being hit with the rod. Manolis, however, was silent except for the few phrases he exchanged with his younger brother. This youngster was going to school and Saitonicolis had great hopes for his progress, in letters, but from the way the child looked at the pastoral attire of his brother and from the questions which he addressed to him, it appeared that he would gladly exchange all his wisdom for Manolis' life of freedom.

Moreover, Saitonicolis, who with heroic libations at the table was feting the happy event for his home, spoke jovially, wishing to encourage the domestic tendencies of his half-wild son, and gently criticized his disobedience on this point: "It was nothing; all children are like that, but when they grow up, they conform and listen to their parents. Nor can they all be literate."

Later he related the story of a shepherd, who, like Manolis, did not for any reason approach other people. He would not even agree to come down to the village for communion. One day, the priest saw him from a distance and shouted to him that he should come down and take communion otherwise his soul would go to Hell. But the shepherd shouted back to him: "Put it in a goatskin flask and send it to me at Maghoulis'," and left. "Very well," said the priest, "I'll show you, you blockhead!" Next day he fills a flask with vinegar and sends it to him. The shepherd, thinking the goatskin contained wine, turns it up and begins to drink, and drink, like a drainpipe, until he feels the vinegar eating up his innards.

With his head bowed, Manolis, who continued to remain silent, laughed at the mishap of his colleague and became bolder with his father, from whom he was separated by feelings of coldness and fear.

Saitonicolis took advantage of the momentary burst of courage to show him that it was time to leave the sheep in order to join the human race. There were shepherds for the sheep; but to supervise and cultivate the land, the old man could not do it alone; one could say that he was not yet an old man, but he was not young either and old age was approaching. In addition, Manolis would also have to provide for a home of his own. He was a man now. And what a man! If all young men like him took off for the mountains to live like wild goats, what would become of the girls? Should they become nuns? Right now the village had such pretty girls, some new sprouts, that one did not know how to choose from among them. "Ah, my son," Saitonicolis shouted out happily, "why couldn't I have your youth?" "You've had your cake, now put your head down!" his wife replied, laughing. Standing beside her son, she encircled him with radiant tenderness and became the interpreter of his silence: "It is another's turn now." And perhaps because the father's hints might have been obscure for the goatish brain of her son, she bent and whispered to him:

"It is the turn of my Manolis, whom we shall marry to a beautiful girl."

Manolis had already understood enough, as the reddening of his face revealed; but when he heard this last statement, his joy and shame aroused in him such a state of confusion, that he pushed his mother away saying:

"I don't want any marriage, and leave me alone, d'you hear!"

Yet, while he was trying to appear angry, a self-betraying smile glowed on his face.

"He doesn't want to get married, he says," Saitonicolis exclaimed laughing, "Say it again, you rascal!"

Manolis hid his face and said with a determination in which joy was dancing:

"I don't want to, I don't want to, I don't want to!"

"All right, don't. Wait till you see the girls and then we'll discuss it again."

Saitonicolis was very pleased because he had come to the conclusion that even if Manolis were driven away, he would never leave the village again. And because of his enthusiasm, he called his wife to bring wine, walnuts, almonds and whatever goods the jars contained. Also, because he was a treasury of anecdotes, (some occasionally salacious,) he recounted one appropriate to the occasion. "Once, a certain man, in order to save his son from bad company, decided to bring him up far away from people, in a remote tower. The youth grew up, became a man, without ever seeing women. Then his father took him and they went to town and he showed it to him from top to bottom. The young man, as innocent as a small child, asked his father about everything he saw: 'what's this' and 'what's that.' When he saw the women, he suddenly stood upright and asked his father what they were. 'These, my son, are demons,' his father told him in order to frighten him, because he saw that they had made a great impression on him. When they returned to their tower, his father said to him: 'Of all the things you saw in town, my son, what did you like best, that I might bring it to you? 'The demons,' the young man answered immediately."

Everybody laughed at the anecdote, and an explosion of laughter escaped from the mouth of Manolis. Because everyone was looking at him, his embarassment flared up and he turned round and round on his chair as if he wanted to fall into the earth, in order to hide himself and his shame. This did not prevent him, however, from acknowledging to himself how right that young man was. Would he not prefer to have such a demon to all the goods of the earth? And yet, he had not the courage to confess it and when the others encouraged him, he lost even more of his courage.

"The same with Manolios," Saitonicolis concluded. "He says he missed us and came to see us. Don't believe him. He came to find his demon. He too wants a demon."

That was too much. When Manolis heard the conclusion and the laughter which accompanied it, he was overcome by such panic that, jumping up, he dashed as if he were a fleeing billy-goat into the interior of the house and, running into his mother who was returning with the wine, he knocked her down and proceeded to conceal himself between the jars.

For a moment everyone was stunned by that sudden flight. Then Saitonicolis, who could not restrain himself from laughing when he saw his wife bent with pain, grimacing, still holding the handle of the shattered container, went near the doorway and shouted towards Manolis:

"Are you crazy?"

"What do you expect with all that talk about demons?" his wife said.

Manolis, who discerned a threat in his father's voice, answered plaintively from his hiding place, as though he were about to cry:

"I don't want you saying things like that to me, or else . . . ."

But he did not finish his threat, because he no longer even dared to think about going back to the mountains and continuing his previous life.

Saitonicolis promised him that he would not tell him anything about demons anymore; he also swore on the bones of the dog, which by the way of euphemism he had substituted in his oaths for the "bones of the Lord."

While Saitonicolina was scolding her husband in a low voice, because he had overdone his joking and upset the lad, Manolis emerged hesitantly and, looking frightened, sat on the floor in a corner, as was his habit. The chair had contributed greatly to his agitation; on it his shame was more exposed to scrutiny.

"It's good that he wasn't sitting next to the front door," Saitonicolina whispered again to her husband, "otherwise he would have set off for the mountains again and then try to catch him."

Saitonicolis smiled at his wife's naiveté: "My dear, he's not leaving; he did not come to leave again. What attracted him to the village this time was something strong, all-powerful." At this point, another anecdote came to his lips: the story of another naive shepherd, who resorted to a doctor to cure him of a strange and irritating malady. And if his daughter's presence had not prevented him, being indifferent as to whether or not his son would again be overcome with panic, he would have have told it. So much the point of the story titillated him.

31

Unable to indulge this whim, he began to describe a plan he had in mind for the humanizing of his son, while Manolis, gaining a little courage, spoke to his brother and, among other things, asked him whether the teacher had used the *falanga* on him too. Saitonicolis in turn was considering all the methods of domestication, one of which was for Manolis to be his proxy as the godfather at a baptism in which he had promised to participate.

* * * * * *

In the morning of the following day, after the liturgy, it did not take much effort to persuade Manolis to take a tour of the village as far as the marketplace with his father. The young man had taken off the woolen clothing of a shepherd; in order to flatter him, his mother dressed him in his father's best clothes, which were a bit too closefitting, even though Saitonicolis was tall and robust.

Thus, he made his formal appearance in the village. We have seen the first impression he made and how Spyridolenia turned it from admiration to derision. Then those who had shortly before seen a youth full of life, to whom the mountains had given the height and the air of a fir-tree, now detected all sorts of amusing imperfections. He was very tall, so much so, that he reminded them of the Saracens,[5] those terrible ghosts of the ruins. With that height, one might think that his head could become dizzy and not be able to remain steady. And in his voice did he not have something of the bleating of a billy-goat? In addition, his sash was carelessly wound around his waist and he did not know how to walk on level ground. His ankles would strike one another and his feet would drag along and roll over the stones in the street, as if the world were coming apart. What a *patouchas!* By the time evening arrived, almost all of the villagers knew him by this nickname and those who saw him during the day confessed with laughter that it hit its mark. Ah, that she-devil, where does she find such things! Like the works of great artists, Spyridolenia's works were easily recognized.

It was true that Manolis, as though he had divined the impression he had made on those women sitting under the great plane tree, was completely disconcerted and seemed to be trying to lessen his enormous height by hiding behind his father. It was the first time he had been exposed to the eyes of so many people. Because of the festive day and the beautiful spring weather, all the villagers were outside, in the doorways, or on the rooftops of their houses, and seemed arranged on both sides of the road deliberately to see him.

Truly, his appearance aroused a tide of curiosity; whatever women remained in their houses ran out to see him. The glances of women bothered Manolis particularly, since it was mainly on them that he wanted to make a good impression, and he had hoped for a triumph, when, in the morning, he saw himself all dressed up in the felt vest and the red sash. Now, however, he thought that he was making a miserable impression and that all the eyes turned on him were mocking him. Consequently, this fear, instead of intensifying his efforts to look presentable, paralyzed him.

Nevertheless, they were welcomed everywhere with friendly greetings.

"It's good to have him back! It's good to have his back!" men and women shouted to the father.

They also addressed various polite expressions to him:

"How are you, Manolio? How did you become such a fine young man? When did you grow so tall?"

More disconcerted was Manolis' dog, who followed him very closely with his tail between his legs, and who was frightened at seeing the dogs of the village before him running about, not to greet him, but in order to attack the rude stranger who entered their kingdom without asking their permission. So much did their attacks distress the wretched animal that, being forced to take shelter between his master's legs, he nearly tripped him. Chasing them away with stones, Saitonicolis was forced to interrupt his conversation with those he met; but after a while the dogs would reappear from other streets, from doors and rooftops, in endless numbers, with continual reinforcements. The path of the father and son through the village was accompanied by wild yelps which increased Manolis' confusion. Seizing a large stone, as though he were an angry titan, he threw it at the dogs. "Cursed be your ancestors! Do you want to eat us?" But instead of hitting the dogs, he almost killed an old man who was sunning his rheumatism.

The road ended between two noisy watermills by a high mill-run. Its walls were covered by moss and bushes and between them the water babbled endlessly. Saitonicolis, accompanied by his son, ran through the rain from the archway at the ditch. When they had passed through they saw five or six *hanoums*[6] stooping near the mill doing their laundry, and they paused there watching the women as they stood in the water with their dresses pulled up above their naked knees, with the white veils thrown down their backs and reaching their haunches. Only one of them drew her veil over her face as though to cover herself.

Another middle-aged woman with a silk veil threaded with damask, was a bit further down at the well hanging out her wash in a row on the bushes of the mill-run. From there she shouted down to Saitonicolis:

"It's good to have him back, neighbor! Is that youth your son?"

"Yes, he's my son, Aisha hanoum," Saitonicolis answered.

"May he bring you joy."

"On my word, may yours bring you joy too."

Manolis paid little attention to the courteous hanoum whom he dismissed as old. His eyes, encouraged by the distance, were turned by preference towards the other side of the mill-run, where he could discern young and pretty faces and where rolled up dresses revealed more to his curiosity. He even dared, as they walked further on, to turn around and look again. And in any case, for him those women were not like the others because they were Turkish.

Nevertheless, the secret glances he shot at the women of his own faith were no less fiery or insatiable. When one middle-aged widow received one such shot right at her breasts, she blurted out: "How he stares! Fire comes out of his eyes."

Saitonicolis, seeing her among the other women, greeted her cheerfully from a distance and asked her what she was doing in another neighborhood, since her house was at the end of the village. What does she hear about her daughter who is in town? May she not stay there! Glory to God that the village has better bridegrooms than the town. And smiling, he indicated Manolis with a gesture.

As they were walking away, he informed his son that that was the widow Zervoudhena, a slightly light-headed woman, "crazy" as he called her, whose daughter had been for quite some time in Kastro with one of her aunts. Saitonicolis loved to tease her, so he thought that if he happened to meet her on the street, he would tell Manolis to kiss her hand, as if she were a respectable old lady, just because she got terribly annoyed whenever people questioned her very questionable youthfulness.

After a few more attacks from the dogs, during which Manolis lost part of his breeches and his dog lost part of an ear, they arrived at the Tsarsi, the market of the village, a short stone-paved street at the center of the Turkish quarter, with stores arranged in a row. Almost all of them were literally general stores, that is to say coffee-shops, taverns, restaurants, grocery and fabric shops all in one.

Here traffic was so lively and the noise so great that it completely confused Manolis, whose knowledge of the area's geography was so limited that he wasn't familiar with many of the parts of the village, including the Tsarsi. But he had a vague idea that here were to be found the wonders of an unknown civilization, which also included another idea, a vaguer and more miraculous one, *the city.* So much was he prepared by his imagination to see amazing things, that everything appeared to him great and wonderful and the hundred or, at most, two hundred persons moving about in the space impressed him as if they were thousands. What contributed to this was the variety resulting from the intermixing of the Turks, old men with big turbans, pipes and red or black shoes, who left their calves naked, and younger ones with Tunisian fezes bordered with a narrow band supporting the bulky blue tassel. A majority of the latter had the same footwear as the Christians, simple high boots or boots slit at the top and tucked tight with their voluminous skirt-trousers so the boots would conform tightly to their calves. What usually distinguished the Turks from the Christians were the lively and open colors of their clothes. In addition, many of the Christians covered the fez with a kerchief of a rather dark color. These "towels" which certain of the distinguished old men wore differed from turbans only in the manner in which they were wrapped. Manolis also remembered a strange detail, which he had observed at church. Many of the old men had shaved their heads in the manner of the Turks, leaving a small tuft at the top. A few years before this hairdo had seemed more common.

Apart from the difference in clothing, there was another difference between Christians and Turks. This one was more profound and resulted from character, which gave the Turks the feeling that they were master -- not absolute and unrestrained as before '21 -- but always maintaining the superiority which came from the authority and pride which they carried through tradition.

The Christians were no longer *rayahs*[7] as they were before '21, but they certainly retained the consciousness of being inferior and the reflection of this feeling could be seen on their faces, no matter how much they tried to conceal it. From the generation which had known the dark years of slavery, so many were still alive that they imparted to the physiognomy of the younger generation something of the gloom and shame of that period, even though these were the same ones who dared to rise against the terrible despot and who paved the way for the relative well being the younger generation now possessed. Due to the courage of those rayahs, the younger people had learned that Turks were not invincible, just as, due to the self-denial and herioism of the rayahs, Turks learned to fear them and take them into account. Yet, two or three of that generation paradoxically persisted in wearing the black kerchief which the Christians were obliged to wear on their heads before '21 as a sign of their servitude and degradation. Perhaps they wanted to give to the younger men a more vivid picture of their time, and also to transmit to them the irreconcilable hatred of the Turks ever vigilant in their hearts.

Indeed Saitonicolis, pointing out to his son one of these old men who was passing by leaning on a walking stick, whispered to his son in a serious tone of voice, in which vengeance throbbed:

"See how the Christians dressed in black during the time of slavery, so that the Turks wouldn't kill them?"

Even though Manolis knew very little about religion, he knew enough about history to understand these feelings which were in his blood, as they were in the blood of all Cretans. Along with his mother's milk he had been suckled with hatred of the Turks and desire for vengeance against them. But his excitement and bewilderment were so great that he did not listen. At that moment, his attention and that of others was drawn to the appearance of a Turk, who very early in the morning had violated Mohammed's commandment, and was staggering through the market, attempting at intervals to strike a heroic pose. With each such attempt, he shouted with a spluttering voice:

"By gosh! I am a man!. . . . I am a *palikari*[8] . . . By the light of Mohammed, I am and I show it."

"What is obvious does not have to be explained. You are the best man of the village, Dervish Agha," standing on either side of the street, the other villagers who were used to seeing him in this condition almost every day, and who also knew that he was the most harmless of all drunkards, used to say to him laughing.

"A whole village is a witness, both the Greeks and Turks . . . that I am a *palikari,*" Agha Dervish said and enthusiastically went his way trying to sing:

If ever I deny my love for you, my frizzy basil,
May mortar, bomb and gunpowder make my skull smooth as a pestle.

He pulled the broad sleeve of his shirt up to his shoulder and exposed his arm to appear more fierce.

Towards the lower part of the market area there was a small square where the private coffee-shops of the Turks were found and the mosque with a half-finished minaret, and across from this a large fountain with a Turkish inscription and iron vessels hanging from chains, so that the passers-by could drink. The Christians avoided drinking from those Turkish goblets in order not to be defiled.

In a low voice Saitonicolis informed his son that the mosque was formerly a church of The Archangel Michael, which, like many other churches, the Turks seized by force when they occupied Crete. Then he showed him the Moudir, who had taken on himself all the authority of the district, both administrative and judicial, and who with a few policemen and volunteers, Moslem and Christian maintained order. The Moudir was an Albanian Turk, one of those left in Crete from the time of Egyptian hegemony, and through whom Moustapha Pasha's iron rule managed to subdue the Cretan Turks and to restore order in Crete. Originally he was a just man; under the Turkish government, however, and through his association with the Turks of Crete, he had become a fanatic and a persecutor of the Christians. In this it seemed that he was following the policy of his government, which, being forced to give privileges to the Christians in 1858, now saw to it that they were nullified.

The Moudir, and the Imam sitting with him in the small shaded court of the mosque, smoked their long pipes, talking in Greek which they seasoned with Turkish words.

From his place, the Moudir could take in with one glance almost the entire village, which began there and spread out to the level of the market and the Turkish neighborhood extending like an amphitheater up the slopes of the mountain, wide and cheerful, like a smiling face, in the midst of a frame created by olive groves and well-watered forests. A row of tall trees, which appeared to rise towards the mountains, followed the meander traced out by the river, an endless rivulet cascading through the village and powering five watermills. On the roofs of the houses there appeared groups of men and women, cheerful against the jovial glittering of the spring sun, directing their glance towards the flourishing valley which spread out below the village, where the shaded gardens and shallow olive-groves were succeeded by an emerald sea of plants, and the ditches crossing each other formed a wonderful abacus from which the water of the streams and the countless springs departed like silvery snakes slipping through the green. Looking there, you could see a receding series of hills and valleys, and further down, a higher plane of mountains split, forming the deep Canyon at the opening of which appeared a hint of the sea, a narrow strip of the Lybian sea. To the west, was a clearing behind the mountains, where the eye could glimpse the wide Mesara valley from which Kofinas rose solitary, isolated in the vagueness of a light mist, a single-peaked mountain where, according to a prophecy ascribed to one "Old Daniel," a calf would swim in the blood shed for the liberation of Crete.

From the valley and the village, from all that area enclosed like a nest, the joy of life rose into the deluge of sunshine and into the harmonious humming of the waters and of the insects mingled with the sound of people conversing from rooftop to rooftop, with the voices of women calling to their children from the heights of the village, with the songs, with the lowing of the cattle and the guardians of the vineyards, with the cawing of blackbirds and with the warbling of nightingales. It was impossible for man to imagine that in this idyllic environment there resided a mortal enmity between two peoples who were divided by religion but not by origin, and who sought an opportunity to fight each other.

Saitonicolis, having guided his son through the market, ended up in the coffee-shop of Smyrnios. The coffee-shop differed from the other stores in the Tsarsi only in the grandeur of its name. It was a small street-level room, with wooden benches all around and shelves higher up, on which were displayed different items of merchandise. It had backless seats, or stools, and a counter on which were placed hookahs,[9] bottles and a long tin pump through which drinks were drawn from the barrels by the inn-keeper. The cafe also had other connected areas for other kinds of merchandise, and an upper floor which was used as a hostel and to which the Turks resorted in order to drink secretly.

The inn-keeper, a lively and untiring short young man with an intelligent face, had lived for several years in Smyrna and was, therefore, named Smyrnios. Returning with a little money and with great intelligence, he devoted himself to his variegated trade. He also knew how to exploit the drunkenness and vanity of the Turks, and, gradually, like mosquitoes, their lands were drowned in wine. He was so obliging that when his clients, the *aghas*,[10] did not have any more money to give him, he would lend them money with interest so that they could continue spending and brutalizing themselves through drunkenness. Moreover, he wasn't afraid of losing the money he lent them, because he had on his side the almost limitless power of the Moudir. Truly, that brutal Albanian had been charmed by the attention and the cunning tongue of Smyrnios, and also perhaps, as it was muttered about, by the favors which only he knew how to render to a Moudir, who loved wine but who did not want to be exposed to the judgment of his fanatic coreligionists. The other Turks had also been seduced by the flattering and obliging manners of Smyrnios. To him, all were *aghas* and *beys*,[11] even Mevloutis the saddle maker.

In order to facilitate his affairs, Smyrnios was also paid in kind, exchanging wine and *raki*[12] for olive oil, fabrics for wheat, herrings and cod for cheese, and needles for eggs which he prepared for his guests whenever he was presented with the need to act as an inn-keeper.

His activity, however, was not restricted solely to the merchantile occupations. On weekdays the Christians, occupied by their work, did not go to the market. It is true that among the Turks there were many who were in constant idleness, and during the day they would go and play checkers and backgammon, while in the evenings they would sit cross-legged on the wooden benches of the coffee-shops, smoking and narrating the events of the war or of the "good old times," as they called the period before '21, amusing themselves with various obscene jokes and monstrous fictions, among which was the story of Doctor Luckmann,[13] the Moslem Faust, who not only healed people but also constructed them. The Turks had separate coffee-shops and went to the Christian ones only to find what they couldn't find at their own: wine. So during week-days Smyrnios opened the cafe for a few hours, as long as was necessary to irrigate his clients, and during the rest of the day he would irrigate his trees and till his fields. While he was working he often reflected that revolutions did not always come about only through guns, but also by hoes and pruning-scissors, by the ell[14] and by the oke.[15]

The assiduousness of the Christians of Crete, while most Turks rotted in idleness and foolishness, brought about a revolution, an enduring one, which slowly yet ceaselessly and surely undermined Turkish rule. Clear proof was right before Smyrnios' eyes. Before the revolution of '21 most of the best lands of the village belonged to the Turks and had mostly been acquired by unjust means. But later, when the rule of force came to an end, the Christians, having secured a small amount of justice from the government, managed through hard work to reacquire a great deal of the land, gradually displacing the Turks, among whom some, no longer owning property and unable to live as they once did from the toil of the rayahs, began to emigrate to the city. Consequently, while the Turkish population dwindled and was gradually losing esteem, the Christian population, on the contrary, grew in numbers and strength. Smyrnios foresaw that conditions would be reversed very soon, and the Turks, in whose fields the Christians had worked until now as laborers or sharecroppers, would find themselves the workers and sharecroppers of their former laborers and slaves.

Also, because of his great longing to see his homeland free, he also desired to see his village free of Turks, imagining that every blow of his hoe was a kick in the backsides of those who were departing.

On account of these ideas, he had an exceptional respect for Saitonicolis, who through his great diligence had increased his property tenfold and, when Smyrnios returned from Smyrna, was found to be among the first landlords of the village. He greeted him with friendly humor, and also addressed compliments to Manolis, who in response overturned a hookah, entangling his feet in the tubes. In any case he could not understand very well what this person who used words uncommon to Crete, was saying. Smyrnios straightened the hookah, smiling and repeating that it was nothing, and the others restrained their laughter with difficulty. Manolis, however, was protected by the presence of his father, who was not one to put up with mocking.

Anyway those present at the cafe were totally absorbed in the excitement of some important news. A letter from Heraklion addressed to Smyrnios, had announced that George, Prince of Denmark, had been proclaimed the new king of Greece. In that remote village of Crete, very little was known, and even less understood, about the events in Athens of the fall of 1861. They had learned that the free Greeks rebelled against King Otto, but such a revolution was incomprehensible to them . . . . so they thought that the expulsion of Otto was the beginning of the abolition of monarchy resulting from the dissension and love of power of the free Greeks. Their sorrow was accompanied by furious indignation. Should all Greeks suffer so much to create this kingdom when those people up there were going to destroy it because of their passions and rivalry? In the minds of the simple villagers, kingdom and King were equated with something indivisible and sacred. Later, other information consoled them. Otto had been expelled because he was not Orthodox, and another King would succeed him on the royal throne, one who was from a great royal family of Europe, and whom the European powers would support in a struggle to regain Constantinople and to replace the cross on Aghia Sophia. These hopes still seemed to the villagers to be possible, since they were confirmed by Tacticos, the interpreter of biblical prophecies. Indeed, his own reckonings presented an approaching time, during which the Turks would be forced to depart for Kokkini Melia. In his books, he found that the liberation of Crete would occur during the year of 1867; according to another prediction, Crete would be liberated only after the retaking of Constantinople -- "The capture of the City, the liberation of Crete"[16] --, therefore, the flight of the Turks for Kokkini Melia would occur in three or four years.

So the news of the election of the new King was doubly cheering: first, because it put to an end to the anxieties which the dethronement of Otto arroused and second, because it presaged the fulfillment of the great hopes of the nation. Of course, nobody who knew the meaning of the prophecies of great hope either talked about these things in the cafes or announced them to any passer-by. They only talked about the new information in hushed voices, since all those present in the cafe were Christians and trusted each other. It was in similar tone of voice that the village elder, Papadosifis, announced it to Saitonicolis, who was sitting next to him.

"God be praised!" Saitonicolis said, overwhelmed and flushed from emotion.

"Good news, hey, Barba[17] Nicolis?" Smyrnios said to him as he approached.

"Yes, God make it so!"

"He will!" You will see."

"But tell me, Sefi," Saitonicolis then asked the village elder sitting next to him, "what kind of a kingdom is this . . . what did you call it?"

"Denmark?"

"Yes, Denmark."

"It is the first time that I hear of it too."

Nobody else knew what and where the homeland of the new King was. Smyrnios, the only one from among the villagers who had gone abroad, found himself wondering about it too. Yet he had confidence that it must be a great kingdom and that the new King was a relative of the czar of Russia.

Suddenly the conversation was brought to a halt by the appearance at the cafe door of a tall, sturdy old man with an unruly beard and prominent eyebrows which gave him the appearance of an aged bandit. He entered coughing, and to his greeting those in the coffee-shop responded:

"Welcome, Mr. Ghiorgaki."

In contrast to his imposing bearing, Ghiorgaki Bereti, nicknamed

Barbarezos, was humble and flattering toward the Turks, seeking their friendship, frequenting their coffee-shops, and using the Turkish words which they mixed with Greek. Sometimes he even greeted them with *mer-haba*.[18] For this the Christians detested him because, rightly or not, there was the rumor that he was used as an informer by the Turks, and as result they were guarded in his presence, though out of fear they treated him kindly.

Barbarezos lived as a Turk, seldom working and waking up late. He was among the few Christians who smoked and always carried a tobacco pouch attached to his belt. He did not go to church regularly and had given up the observance of fasting, something which aroused immeasurable dismay and repugnance. From the Turks he had also acquired the rude habit of sitting uninvited at others' tables.

While Barbarezos accommodated himself on the sofa, Smyrnios presented two cups of coffee to Saitonicolis and his son. What he expected, though, was for Manolis to drink the coffee with one sip and then gape in pain, did not happen because Saitonicolis, foreseeing this, whispered to his son in time:

"Drink it sip by sip because it's hot. Do you hear?"

Then Barbarezos saw Manolis and congratulated his father.

"Well done, Koubare[19] Nicolis. May you be proud of your son. He looks like he is becoming a double man."

"The father is a man, and the son is a man," Saitonicolis said, laughing.

"He is the image of your late father, Koubare Nikolis. I believe I am looking at him . . . And tell me, my son," he said to Manolis with his most courteous smile, "what good thing did you bring us from the sheepfold? *Mizithra*,[20] goat's milk?"

"I didn't bring anything," Manolis answered, in ecstasy being distracted by the little mirrors hanging in a row from the shelf of the cafe, moving and forming different playful combinations of light.

"You shepherds," Barbarezos said almost plaintively, "don't love the dairy products because you have them every day and you think that we don't love them either."

Leaving the subject of dairy products, he returned to the recollection of Manolis' grandfather, who was killed during the grand revolution. He wove him an inflated encomium, fabricating with indirect flatteries an invasion of the luxurious home of Saitonicolis. He and Sifakas were the stoutest warriors of '21. And he had such a voice that when the Turks heard him shout "stop you *bourmades!*"[21] they were terrified. At Gerapetro he went up to the walls with Zervonikolas, and if the others had followed them and had not lost courage, they could have taken the fortress. During the great battle of Kritsa, he killed five Misirlides[22] with his own hand. In fact, where did he not fight? He even went to the Morea with other Cretans.

"On your word, Mr. Ghiorgaki did you ever fight?" Saitonicolis asked him with a slight smile.

"I did what I could," Barbarezos answered, unassumingly.

"You don't remember me because you were still young, but why don't you ask the Captain?"

The Captain, a serious and laconic old man sitting opposite, who seemed to be paying more attention to the noise of his worry beads than to Barbarezos' speeches, most probably had this title given to him during the Egyptian rule, when, before the revolution, he became rich as a sub-prefect. But he had fought in '21 and could be useful as a witness.

"Can I remember, now after so many years, what each pasha did?" he said, with the pleasure of a man who was forced to lie.

"I thought, Mr. Ghiorgaki," said Smyrnios turning away from the door where he was washing his hookahs, "that in '21 you were a child."

"I was born during the great darkness. Figure. From 1797 to 1827 what do we have?"

"Twenty-four. So you were twenty-four years old?"

"Right."

The memory of the "great darkness" appeared to have electrified the Captain.

"I remember the great darkness," he said. "I must have been eight years old."

Everybody turned with attention and great curiosity towards the old man; Smyrnios also stopped his work in order to listen.

"I was down in the meadows," the Captain recounted, "when suddenly, at noon, the world began to darken, and it became dark, as if night had fallen. I looked at the sun and saw a black spot and around it stars. As if it were night, didn't I tell you? And the oxen began bellowing and the dogs cried. I was with my mother, god rest her soul, and she said to me: 'Make the sign of the cross, my child, make the sign of the cross, my child,' She too made the sign of the cross and was entreating God and the Virgin Mary. There were other villagers in the meadow, Christians and Turks; and you could hear the wailing of the people and the sounds of the animals all at the same time. Everybody thought that the world was coming to an end."

"The sun must have gotten caught; isn't that so, Captain Dimitris?" Smyrnios said.

"It must have. Do I understand these things?" the Captain answered.

Hence, having an excuse, they talked about other similar natural phenomena and of the great earthquake, which had completely ruined Heraklion several years ago. Nikolakis Stivaktis, whom they ironically called "Astronomos," because he had the curiosity of a naturalist and the aspiration to be a meteorologist, forecasting the weather and the harvests, expressed the opinion that the earthquakes originated from the "metal of the earth," without being able to explain clearly what this metal was. But Saitonicolis, apologetically remarked that he should not say these things which were complete nonsense again. And he cried out because such words, after all, were a sin. Earthquakes are divine wrath brought about by the sins of men. This was verified by Anagnostis Ksinias, citing the testimony of David: "He that ruleth over men must be just, ruling in the fear of God." Astronomos, who lacked Galileo's talent for recantation, thought that it would be best to postpone his modern ideas for a more appropriate time.

This pause was anticipated impatiently by Skizomichelis, a rustic fellow in shepherd's clothing, who appeared to be amazed at how good people paid attention to the words of this "crazy man," Astronomos. The important question for him was the loss of one "barren nanny goat." And he asked Manolis if he had happened to see her. Her marks were "red-eyed, black, striped, ear-marked."

While he was saying this, he was observing Manolis, as if he suspected that the disappearance of the nannygoat was his doing. Why not? Do not all shepherds steal? They steal ten sheep from you; you steal ten more from somebody else, and he in turn steals some more; in this way a kind of equilibrium is maintained.

Because it concerned things about which Manolis was a specialist, he answered boldly that he had not seen the nanny-goat, that it had been a long time since he had seen a lost goat. Apparently, guessing Skizomichelis' suspicion, he reinforced his words with an oath:

"God forbid!"

* * * * * *

After noon, Saitonicolis guided his son to their fields near the village. In the afternoon, when they were returning, they met again on the road the village elder Papadosifis and continued the conversation about things in general, which Barbarezos' arrival at the cafe had interrupted.

"I believe," Papadosifis said to him, "that very soon we will have a revolution. Smyrnios' letter says that at Chania they are not getting along well with Pasha Ishmael; he is an anti-Christian fighter like Housni."

"Right! He, too, will leave like Housni," Saitonicolis said. "The Cretans will send him to old man devil, the way they did Veli Pascha."

"Yes, but if the Sultan does not agree to remove him, what'll happen?"

"War," Saitonicolis answered. "Don't Tacticos' papers say so?"

"How do I know?" Papadosifis said, scratching his forehead.

"Listen to what I am telling you, Koubare! The end of Turkey is near and you remember that for me."

"May God provide! But how can I know for sure? We thought it was certain in '41. Let it be."

Later Papadosifis mentioned that Ishmael Pasha, like his predecessor, appeared to be trying to nullify the privileges which the Cretans had acquired during the revolution of '58, especially the right to have weapons. This and the taxation had created great exasperation among the populace of Chania.

"Listen to the sounds at Chania, listen as they get closer," said Saitonicolis, repeating a proverbial phrase.

When they arrived in the village, the sun had already set and the new moon had appeared; the women, staring at it fixedly, made the sign of the cross saying:

> To you, new moon, I send a prayer,
> And Him who created you, I praise.

Saitonicolis, looking up at a window, discerned among the basil and the carnations the beautiful face of a girl who was watering her flowers. He saluted her with affectionate intimacy:

"Good evening, Pighio."

"Good evening to you, Barba Nicolis," a fresh and spirited voice answered from the window. "Welcome to your son, too, whom we rarely see."

"The basil is beautiful, Pighio," Saitonicolis said. "Won't you throw us a sprig?"

"With pleasure," the girl answered, and in a moment her sunburned hand reached out from among the flower-pots holding a bouquet of basil and carnations.

"Here you are, Barba Nicolis."

"Flowers are for the young," Saitonicolis said smiling and pushed Manolis forward who, raising his arms almost to the window, caught the flowers in the air, blushing, but also pleased with his daring.

Manolis arrived home, overcome with fatigue and feeling dazed. When running in the mountains he never got as tired as he did from all the excitement of that day and from the crowd and the succession of impressions. The noise of the village and the market-place still buzzed in his ears and the sharp smell of the merchandise and of Smyrnios' hookahs followed him. It was as though he were intoxicated. But in that giddiness, he could hear whispers of the sweetest and fairest promises. The enchanting phantoms which he had seen in the reveries of his solitude, appeared again, more substantial in that inebriation, and his soul was flooded with joy ready to overflow, to pour out in songs, in crazy shouts, in confessions.

But it was only to his dog that he dared confess part of his happiness and his hopes. In order to avoid the fuss of that morning, they did not take him with them for the afternoon walk. When Manolis saw him again he embraced him effusively and said to him:

"We're not going to the mountains again, ay, Three-Eyes? It's good here in the village . . . there are beautiful girls too. Did you see Pighio, who had the basil and the black eyes? . . . We are not going to the mountains again, hey Three-Eyes?"

But Three-Eyes did not seem to share in his idea. It was not even possible for the dog to be pleased in a place where he found only enemies.

So he accepted his master's endearments gloomily. At least this was what Manolis thought and said to him:

"What! Don't you like the village?"

And after watching him for a few moments, as though he realized for the first time that Three-Eyes was not human, he said to him again:

"If you were Manolis, you would like it; but you are only a dog, poor fellow! What can I possibly do for you?"

3

Two weeks later, the baptism of the daughter of Moustovasilis, a well-to-do young villager, took place; and the god-father was, according to his father's plan, Manolis.

For days his female relatives discussed what name to give his god-daughter, finally agreeing to name her Aglaia; everybody liked this name so much that even Saitonicolina gave up her right, as the mother of the god-father, to insist preference be given to her own name, the difficult to pronounce name, "Reginia."[23] When one of Manolis' aunts suggested Aglaia it sounded strange. But when she informed them that Smyrnios had given the name to one of his god-daughters several days before, Saitonicolina's initial grimace was transformed into an approving smile. Then it appeared "noble" and beautiful to all. Smyrnios had brought it from "above," or as we would say today, "from Europe." With that one word those villagers, who had never gone abroad, named the civilized world with which they were not familiar and simply imagined to be wonderful. Smyrnios, who had gone abroad, was considered a representative of that civilization and consequently a superior man, whose preference and choice could be used as criteria of reliability, good taste and sound judgment. But his prestige could also be attributed to his true virtues. Had he been a sluggard or a rustic, his language would have provoked laughter, like Astronomos' theories, and his short jacket with the waist-high open pleat in the back would have seemed a clown's costume.

The more the women repeated the new name, the more they discovered grace and refinement in its gentle sound and brilliance.

Only Saitonicolis, when he heard it, grimaced with contempt and said to his wife:

"Alas, what sort of name is that, for the poor child?"

But he did not insist, paying little attention to such trivial things.

That evening there was a great deal of activity in Moustovasilis' house. All of his women relatives were there, busy going back and forth preparing the baptismal dinner. There, too, was Pighio, first cousin of the young housewife, a tall and blossoming eighteen-year-old, with a girlish innocence in her eyes, voice and laughter. Pighi's face was crimson-colored from hunching her tall body over the low fire frying mizithra pitas which filled the house with a pleasant aroma. Five or six scantily clad children, who were standing barefoot or sitting around, and a black cat greedily watched the rose-colored pitas accumulate in pyramids on large trays. While she turned the pitas over in the frying pan and put new ones in the noisily boiling olive-oil, Pighio also kept an eye on the cat and, at intervals, pushed her back with the tongs. She gave a pita to each child, laughing at their insatiable appetites and the comic grimaces with which they gulped down the hot pastry. But later, seeing that there was no end to their childish gluttony, she said:

"Children, the god-father says that whoever eats more than one pita before he comes from church will not receive a baptismal favor.

And poking at the fire, she asked with a sly smile if any of the children wanted another pita. The children, not having the strength to restrain their appetites, yet afraid of losing the baptismal favors, restricted themselves to ambiguous refusals accompanied by lengthy smackings of the tongue against the palate.

In a way, the house reflected the care of a young housewife who had not yet been overwhelmed by life's ordeals. The relatively new house and furniture indicated that Moustovasilis' household was only three or four years old. The house consisted of two large rooms on the first floor, the inner one of which was used mainly as a storeroom. There was also a room upstairs, but the life of the small family was restricted to the room facing the street, which was spacious enough to be used as a living room, bedroom and kitchen. One of the corners toward the back had a large, nuptial bed, with colorful bedspreads which looked like used as curtains. Along most of the entire length of one wall, there projected a long beam, a piece of wood below the rafters, from which hung, in orderly fashion, a variety of rugs and clothing. The shelf on the opposite wall was decorated with objects of showy array: vessels with different pictures, colored ornaments, paniers and baskets made of straw, all childhood knick-knacks belonging to the lady of the house. Beneath the shelf, under both windows, were Moustovasilis' guns and a row of white cloths displaying their varied borders.

Further on, one observed the ample fireplace with its arch, its niches and shelves for cooking utensils, a small cupboard and a jug stand next to the door at the end of the wall, from which the necks of the jugs, sealed with "jug spines," and the pitchers protruded like guns. The water dripping from the jug stand had begun to form puddles on the dirt floor.

The roof was supported by thick beams in the middle, crossed by beams and rafters of cedar and cypress wood which, being unfinished and recently stripped off the bark, still retained and gave off their aroma. From them dangled various ropes from which in the fall, strings of fruit preserved for winter hung like chandeliers; now only cheese and goat's milk appeared suspended in the air between two boards on ropes interwoven with thorns to prevent an invasion of mice from the roof.

The Dutch door opening on the street had a little mirror hanging next to it. Though the lower half was shut, the upper door was open. Through it, street noise entered - the tramping of villagers returning from the fields with their cattle, the shouts of shepherds and their cursing of the bulls fighting in the middle of the street: "Here you ox, here! Go to the devil!" The barking of dogs gradually faded away along with the rest of the noise.

Meanwhile a pig, unable to sleep because of the varied and enticing aromas coming from the house, besieged the door, rattling it with his snout like some batttering ram and grunted with growing indignation, as if he were saying, "Come on, open up, already!"

Nobody paid attention to him; the women were so busy with their preparations that they did not even hear those annoying grunts - to which, moreover, they were accustomed. The furniture and the household goods were inadequate for this special occasion, so tables and chairs were borrowed from the neighbors. They tried to arrange the tables to form a big enough table for all the guests. Precious trays were brought down and the napkins were taken from the shelf to be set on the table. All this was being done feverishly, with noisy confusion, because those who went to church for the baptism were expected to return at any moment. At the last moment, they noticed that the three oil lamps were not enough, and one of the female relatives, going out to get a fourth one, collided with the pig attempting to rush in.

Pighi, having completed her task, was still sitting in front of the hearth whose reflection surrounded her figure with a rosy brightness. Due to the heat she felt a languor in her limbs, a gentle loosening of the muscles, which made her eyelids droop. Tiny beads of perspiration shone like diamond dust on the hint of down which could barely be discerned, like a transparent shadow, on her upper lip. Rather than making her unattractive, it gave her, on the contrary, a special charm. Sitting thus with her fore-arms idle in her lap, still holding the fork with which she turned the pitas, she appeared to be smiling at a beautiful dream which her half-shut eyes saw in the depths of the fire, in the dance and play of the flames.

The children, sitting around her on the floor, also seemed lost in anticipation. But they still jealously kept an eye on the suspicious movements of the cat, which had turned her green eyes towards a mouse running noisily across the beams of the roof. The mouse changed direction toward the pyramids of pitas, thinking the guards had fallen asleep. At the very moment it attempted an assault, five simultaneous "psits" turned it to flight.

Pighi got up and said to the youthful lady of the house:

"It's getting late, Garifalio, and nobody has come to tell us what they named her."

As was the custom, the Saitonicolis' family had kept secret the name which Manolis would give to his goddaughter; and the women, occupied with the preparation of the banquet, were trying to guess what it was.

At that moment hurried footsteps of barefoot children were heard and a girl's crimson face appeared at the upper door. Unbolting the latch with difficulty, she opened the door and rushed in with a swarm of other children.

"They named it Achladia,[24] Aunt Garifalio," they all shouted in unison, as if they were announcing the victory at Marathon.

Garifalio looked at the children with disbelief. They must not have heard right. But the children insisted. One of Moustovasilis' aunts grimaced with displeasure. Wouldn't it have been better if they named it "cherry tree," or "peach tree?" What a name! Garifalio, in order to restrain the old woman's tongue, said that the children must certainly have misunderstood. And even if it were the name, so long as the child had a long life, what it was named did not bother her.

"He must have named it Aglaia, you'll see," said Pighi, who knew the new name Smyrnios brought from "up there."

The conversation was interrupted by a terrible grunt of triumph. Having found an opportunity, the pig rushed in and, advanced towards the table with piggish insensitivity. Horrified, all the women shouted "oust!" and Pighi, grabbing a stick, pursued him with merciless whacks and shut the door again, shouting:

"A jinx on you, filthy pig!"

A little later, another messenger confirmed the children's announcement: at the window appeared an old neighbor, who had been present at the baptism and had also heard that the child was named Achladhi.[25]

"Long live the newly christened child."

And in fact something like this had happened. Because Manolis found it difficult to retain that unusual name in his memory, his sister, after many vain attempts, told him to have in mind "achladia" in order to remember it. But when the moment came for him to say it to the priest, he found in his memory only "achladia," slightly changed. And the priest, to whom the pear tree was also more familiar, began to repeat the name in his blessings, just as Manolis said it to him. Why should it sound strange to him since he had heard baptismal names such as Melia[26] and Triantaphylia?[27] With his nasal chant echoing in the dome, the distortion was not detected, so it was a bit late when the godfather's sister and mother noticed it.

The first immersion in the font had been made and the priest was baptizing "the servant of God Achladia," when Saitonicolina approached him and said in a hesitating voice:

"Aglaia is the name, Reverend Father, Aglaia."

The priest interrupted the baptism and holding the wailing infant in the air, answered:

"Aglaia, Achladia, it's the same thing. What do I know about the kind of names you go out and find?"

And he started to submerge the child once more, but Saitonicolina insisted, contradicting her husband, who, displeased, said to the priest:

"Go on with your work, my good man, and don't listen to anybody."

Manolis also thought that the name was Aglaia. But why did they not ask his sister, who knew better? At that moment he had a more serious preoccupation; he was observing unfamiliar anatomical details of the infant writhing in the priest's hands.

Moustovasilis, finally became angry, and shouted that they should name it whatever they wanted, but just not upset his child excessively.

The priest made the decision and performed two more immersions, baptizing "the servant of God, Aglaia."

Barbarezos, who was never absent from church when the service was followed by a dinner, stood next to Moustovasilis and approved the latter's words. With this wrangling, the child was in danger of catching cold . . . perhaps the food was too. The world would not end because of a name. But the Reader Ksinias, nicknamed Tereres, grimaced while chanting to indicate that he felt a serious error had been committed.

Meanwhile various villagers, seeing light in the church, came in and stood around in their woolen fezes. If Manolis had not been busy with his duties as a godfather, he would have recognized, among those who had come in last, an old friend.

The church was newly built and the interior half finished. There were no pews; attached to the temporary altar screen of unvarnished wood were old icons, bearing traces of destruction and desecration which the old church had suffered under the Turks during the great revolution. From the dome, two painted heads of white stone with long black moustaches made threatening faces; each had a ring in its mouth, from which the chandelier would hang. Swallows, having entered through open skylights, added their nests to these statues as if they were caps. Wakened by the chanting, the birds began flying inside the church with small cries of surprise.

The baptismal ceremony was already coming to an end, and Astronomos, who was performing the duties of sexton that evening, took away the font; meanwhile Manolis, who had handed his goddaughter over to the midwife, was watching with curiosity the shiny head of Barbarezos, who was the only bald man among the villagers. Then, looking up at the dome, he noticed that Barbarezos' bald head was directly below the swallows' nest. Imagining something that could quite possibly happen, namely that a wet glob of something might fall with a smack on that smooth pate, he started laughing.

Suddenly his mirth ceased, his eyes opened wide and retreated a step, as if he were seeing a horrible apparition. Before him stood the teacher, the terrifying monk, unchanged, the only difference being that he was approaching Manolis with a smile in order to greet him. Manolis, wanting to flee, cried out, gasping as if he had run miles,

"Go away! Don't come near me!"

Grasping a heavy ecclesiastical book from a nearby window, he raised it menacingly, and the echo from the holy dome repeated the blasphemy with horror:

"May the devil take your ancestors![28]

Those present, particularly amazed at that blasphemy inside the church, had already intervened. Saitonicolis, disarming his son, whispered to him in a voice trembling with anger:

"You dog, what have you done?"

He also told the teacher to leave. Look at what he did with spankings and the falanga! He is to blame!

At the same time Saitonicolina had approached and with a calm voice told her son that he had committed a great sin.

"How is it that God did not pour down fire to burn us, my son!"

Manolis listened to her, bowing his head on the verge of tears. Even he did not know how such a thing had happened to him.

"Shame, my child," his mother said to him in a low voice. "Imagine your becoming frightened and losing your wits as though you had seen the devil. As though the teacher were a monster and could eat people. And I was so happy thinking that you would become a good man, like your father, and be the first in war, like your grandfather. Oh, the shame, when others will say you are a coward, my son!"

Everybody was shaken by the incident, and most of all Moustovasilis. These were not good signs; he was quite fearful for his child and his household in general. His fears and agitation were reinforced by Tereres, who insisted that the baptism had not been executed canonically, and that it therefore was the reason the sacrilegious incident had taken place.

The priest was terribly angry. Where did Manolis think he was? Saitonicolis meekly beseeched him not to scold Manolis for fear of frightening him again. When Manolis, following his mother's advice, approached the priest and asked his forgiveness, kissing his hand, the priest admonished him gently. Only Barbarezos attributed no significance to the event and encouraged Manolis. "Come on now, it is not the end of the world. God is not an Albanian. A pure heart is enough."

The teacher meanwhile had disappeared. The rest of them returned to the house, where the congratulations and the sight of the groaning table dispersed the chill of the unpleasant episode.

Barbarezos, without losing time on formalities, sat down at the table facing the priest; then he called the others to seat themselves, as if he were master of the house. A separate table had been set for the women in the inner house. Only two or three would stay in order to serve the men; among them was Pighi.

The priest blessed the food and drink and the feast began. But the master of the house, even if he tried to appear happy, was tormented by the idea that his child's baptism had not been performed properly. Finally, he could restrain himself no longer and questioned the priest. The priest became angry. A baptism which he himself had performed was not canonical? "Who says such things?" he said, looking sideways at Tereres, because he knew the latter was both openly and secretly fighting him, having an eye on one of his two parishes so that he, too, might become a priest.

And truly, Tereres was maintaining, openly by now, that, since the child had been baptized with two names, the baptism was not performed according to the procedures of the Church. Instead it was Frankish.[29] The Church prescribes three immersions in the name of the Father, the Son and the Holy Spirit; but, for the real name of the child, there had been only two immersions. The first one had been for the non-existent name Achladia. Therefore it was as though it had not happened, and the infant was not baptized in the name of the Father. After Tereres had demonstrated his theological superiority and the ignorance of the priest, he also expressed fear that when the bishop found out what had happened, the event would have consequences for the priest.

The priest did not in good conscience consider the incident a serious mistake; but the sophistic indictment by his antagonist put him in a difficult position. However, just as he was prepared to become angry and tell Tereres straight out that the latter was saying these things because he wanted his parish and that Tereres should put this ambition out of his mind because the bishop would never ordain a man who reads the Book of Solomon, a brilliant idea came to him and by sophistry he silenced the sophist:

"Why don't you go and shear sheep?" he asked him.

The baptism, said the priest, was most canonical since the two names presented an extremely small difference: Aglaia and Achladia were the same thing. Thus the Virgin Mary was sometimes called Mariam and sometimes Maria, and Moises was called Moses.

Triumphantly the priest exclaimed:

"Why don't you tell us that the Virgin Mary -- God forgive me -- and Moses were improperly baptized so that you can show yourself a true Free-Mason?"

Tereres could not find anything to oppose in this argument, and kept silent because, frightened as he was by the priest's last words, he would have unpleasant results if he got more irritated.

In fact, Tereres did not have a good reputation. Because he was the son of a mandrake,[30] who, it was rumored, worshipped evil spirits, an idea was circulating that along with the occult books of his father he also inherited relations with the Devil. By virtue of this reputation, which made his scrawny ugliness repugnant, he could not find a wife and was approaching the age of forty as a bachelor, though he was one of the most prosperous villagers. For this reason, the bishop refused to ordain him, even though he was not unsuitable in other respects, since he knew how to read and write, (as much as was considered necessary), and could chant. He had a high opinion of his chanting, which the others did not share, and because of his funny twittering, they called him Tereres. So, when he saw that the priest was ready to cast the accusation of witchcraft in his face, in order to finish him off, Tereres hastened to back down. While on one hand, out of excessive religious zeal, he attempted to deny the accusation, on the other he reinforced such suspicions by insisting out of avarice on exercising the therapeutic part of his father's craft. That is to say, he made amulets for those who suffered from diseases of the nerves, and he gave out "prescriptions," which the patients would place on their necks in order to get rid of fevers or would dissolve them in water and drink them to cure other maladies. While it is true that this kind of therapy was commonly used and that others wrote similar prescriptions —— curing the mumps by writing five alphas on the swelling and reading Saint Cyprian over the sick, —— nobody else had the suspicious paternal tradition of Tereres.

Moustovasilis, cheering up because of the outcome of the discussion, drank to the godfather's health:

"I'm glad to have you here, Koubare Manolio."

"Welcome to my family, Koubare," answered Manolis who, with the help of the wine, had already forgotten the frightful glance which he thought Christ had shot at him from the altar screen in the church.

The priest put an end to the discussion with Christian forebearance, and began to chant, "All those who are baptized in Christ." The others repeated the hymn, while Manolis, succumbing to the common impulse, chanted it according to the priest's prompting, but with such humorous distortions and with such a loud voice, that the children sleeping on the bed woke up frightened and began to cry, while those at the table struggled to restrain themselves from laughing, and leaned towards the person sitting next to him and whispered:

"Doesn't he have the voice of a billy-goat?"

The only one who did not try to hide his smile was Tereres. In order to antagonize him, the priest said that Manolis had a very good voice and that if he knew how to read and write, he could become a great chanter. Barbarezos, pushing up the ante for purposes of flattery, swore that for a moment he had been deluded; he thought he was listening to Drakakis, the first chanter of Kastro![31] The priest did not reach such a level of hyperbole, but he did not consider it necessary for Manolis to be literate in order to become a chanter, as long as his ear could catch the modes.[32] After all, Sykologos the builder, though he was totally illiterate, could chant well enough when others read for him.

Tereres laughed. "Oh, yes! He chanted so well that he made a salad of all the modes and he would say one thing for another when he could not hear the reader well.' Once the reader said 'the aspirations of the world' and he sang 'the ass of the world' as if the world were a donkey. If I were a priest, I would not permit the builder to chant, because, after all, it would be mocking the divine."

"Let's see your honor become a priest, and then prevent him," said the priest, becoming stubborn again. "I believe he chants well and correctly, better than some who think they are somebody and that nobody else is."

This new dispute was interrupted by Manolis, who, in order to show that he was not so ignorant as they thought, suddenly began to sing "Christ is risen," raising his voice to its fullest. If there had happened to be glass in the windows, they surely would have been shattered by the vibrations of that stentorian voice.

Manolis enthusiastically drank to the health of the Koubara and clinked his glass with hers.

"May you live a thousand years, Koubare!" Garifalio answered. Similar toasts endlessly crossed back and forth:

"Long live the newly baptized child!"

"May he that anointed with oil, also plant the vineyard.[33]

"Here's to the joys of the unmarried ones!"

In a little while, the wine brought the merriment to its peak.

Only Tereses was silent and gloomy, not so much reacting to his defeat, as to another defeat which he foresaw. Besides having his eye on the parish, he had an eye on Pighi, so that he would become a priest, and she a "presbytera."[34] Gathering from the furtive glances which Manolis let fly at Pighi every time they wished him the joys of marriage, and from the blushing with which Pighi received those glances, Tereres began to fear that all along the line his plans were in danger. His fears were reinforced by the persistence with which the girl's glance avoided his, while he saw it repeatedly directed towards Manolis.

The forks had been put down and the glasses were going back and forth, touching each other with great liveliness; because those who drank considered it necessary to accompany each glass with a toast, they now toasted everyone, from the dead ancestors to the latest sprouts of the two families which were linked by baptism. The excuses to drink were endless. From time to time they were directed towards Pighi:

"To the joys of marriage, Pighio!"

"To your joys!" the maiden answered without affectation.

After a while the confusion typical of drunkenness came about. While the priest chanted, an old man at the end of the table, who had gone to Karpathos during the revolution, was imitating the Karpathian accent, and those around him were laughing their hearts out. On the other side, Astronomos was telling how a Frankish ship had come to shore a few days before and picked up various marble pieces from the ruins of an ancient city there. Thus, they were given a pretext to wonder why on earth the Franks wanted the idols and the other ancient marble pieces, which they sought while touring the island. Some suspected that these travellers were a bit idolatrous, while others said that inside the idols there was gold, which the Franks knew how to extract. This was proved by the fact that someone had found a golden statue. As for the marble pieces with inscriptions, Astronomos was certain that the letters on them had led those foreigners to the discovery of treasures. He too had discovered one such inscribed tablet some time ago, but he made the mistake of showing it to a red-bearded Frank passing through the village.

While they were talking about these things, the door opened and in came a villager, a relative of the master of the house, who had just arrived from Heraklion. All turned towards him to learn the news from the city. Sure enough, the villager told them about something fascinating which stirred up the whole city of Heraklion those days. A few days before, all the Moslem inhabitants of a village in Pediada had entered the city, following a monk from Mount Athos chanting "Christ is risen." They had gone to the Cathedral and, presenting themselves to the Archbishop, announced their decision to return to the Christian religion, the faith of their fathers. The Turks of the city, seeing what was going on, became furious, and the Pasha ordered the arrest and imprisonment of the villagers and the monk.

The Christians asked for and succeeded in getting the intervention of the consuls,[35] who appealed to religious freedom, which had been declared under Hatihoumayoun.[36] The Pasha, after trying in vain, by way of threats, tortures and promises to reconvert the villagers, was forced to free them; but he exiled the monk, in spite of the fact that he was from Crete. The monk, was named Maridakis and came from the region of Rethymnon. Because he had involuntarily killed a

Christian several years back, he went to Mount Athos and became an ascetic; he had returned from there recently and had begun to teach, in an attempt to lead the Mohammedans of Crete back to the religion their ancestors had abandoned.

The women, who had approached and were listening to what was being said, made the sign of the cross whispering:

"Glory be to God!"

The men were no less excited. The noisy drunkenness of a few minutes before seemed to have been dispelled at once. The priest's voice lifted, as if in a paean of victory, and he chanted, "A Great God, our God." The hymn ended, then Astronomos, lifting up his glass in a movement like that of a man ready to shoot his rifle from sheer enthusiasm, called out with a trembling voice:

"To the health of all Greeks!"

"Viva!" the others responded with one voice.

"And next year without the curse!" Moustovasilis added, expressing through word-play the wish "without the curs," that is, without Turks.

"Amen!"

"See how Tactikos' words have started to come true?" Saitonicolis said to the priest.

No longer taking into account Barbarezos' presence, Saitonicolis drank to the health of one destined to fulfill the great hopes of the nation:

"May we rejoice in our new King!"

Even Barbarezos -- who after all was a Christian too -- was not unmoved. In fact, he was so moved, that, carried away by the inebriation of the wine, he began to cry, remembering one of his younger brothers, who had been taken captive during the revolution and not been seen since.

Saitonicolis said to him in a loud voice that this was the hour of joy, not lamentation. Turning towards Pighi, he told her cheerfully:

"Isn't that so, Pighi?"

Then he began to sing:

> The apple, hanging on the sweet apple-tree,
> ripens, shrivels up, or is eaten by passers-by.
> This is how the maiden is once she comes of age .....

And he finished with an exclamation:

"Ah! youth where have you gone!"

Saitonicolis was also enthusiastic because he saw that his plan for the domestication of his son was succeeding. The wine had sufficiently loosened up Manolis' tongue, so that he was able to say, like the Satyr of ancient comedy:

Whence ever did I find
this griefless cure of shame.

In fact, he had grown so bold that his insistent glances embarassed Pighi. The truth is that in her innocence she did not see in Manolis any of the imperfections which, in their malevolence, others had detected. She could only see the son of Christian parents, the young, vigorous, strong man who could with one punch smash the puny Tereres, who was sweet on her.

In the meantime, Astronomos, who knew or guessed the feelings of Tereres, amused himself by vexing his jealousy:

"My good man, can't you see? he whispered to him; "Patouchas, whom we took for a blockhead, has made a match with Pighio."

"I believe you are drunk and see one thing for another," Tereres said, pretending to be indifferent.

"Listen to what I'm telling you. Open your eyes and you'll see their eyes playing like the stars . . . there, did you see her, how she smiled at him?"

Tereres changed color from yellow to green.

"Eh! And what do I care after all?" he said. "She's not my sister."

"Come on now, you act as though you don't care . . . You are unmarried too and Pighio is a good and pretty bride. Just look at her; all the roses of May are blossoming on her cheeks. And a real woman, a veritable frigate."

Tereres could not drown a sigh.

"But are you telling the truth, does she want him or is she just playing with him?" he said after a few minutes.

"Don't you have eyes to see? Lord have mercy!"

"She's thrown herself at that ox!"

"Why is she throwing herself at him? For his youth. What else do you expect? The young man with the young girl and the old folk have a good heart."

At that moment Manolis, as if he were seized by a sudden frenzy, clinked his glass with so much force, that he smashed it, transported with joy, cried out:

"He who put on the oil, should add the vinegar."

"Let it become oil and vinegar dressing!" Astronomos added, all the while laughing noisily.

Afterwards, the godfather got up and with an unsteady step went round the table giving out baptismal favors. When he came to where

Pighi was standing, he whispered to her, while giving her as many of the twenty-drachma coins as his hand could take from the purse he held:

"I thank God, Pighio!"

The girl was shaken and with a faint voice she replied:

"May you live a thousand years!"

After a little while the priest got up and everybody else imitated him.

It was time to leave. Pighi had already prepared a "papyrus," wrapping cloth around a piece of wood and dipping it in olive oil. Then, having ignited it, she offered it to Saitonicolis, who went out first, lighting up the road for his family and relatives. Manolis followed, staggering and delirious from drunkenness. When they approached their home, he bent toward his mother and said to her, trying to lower his voice:

"Oh, if you can believe it . . . I'm going to marry Pighio."

4

"Didn't I tell you?" Saitonicolis said smiling when the next day he learned of Manolis' confession from his wife. "He came to find a demon for himself, but he's lucky and has found an angel."

Even if his son's choice was premature, Saitonicolis liked it. Perhaps, it could be included in the father's future plans. He cherished a special friendship and esteem for Pighi, perhaps because she reminded him of his wife, as Reginio was when he had fallen in love with her. Pighi for him was the ideal woman, good housekeeper and a good worker in the fields. Since her mother's death a year ago, she had managed to replace her in caring for the house and in helping her father and brother in their farm work. Saitonicolis loved and admired work to such an extent that he thought women were enobled by a mattock; and he became enthusiastic when he saw her harrowing like a man, following her brother's plough.

In harvesting she surpassed the men in speed and endurance. All rosy-red under the broad scarf, which protected her face from the sun, she harvested four times as much as the others.

And, in the most arduous work, she kept her natural cheerfulness and laughter, which reminded Saitonicolis of a song from his youth:

Whenever you speak
blossoms fall and when you
smile roses.
My light, I have seen your elegance in no other.

Saitonicolis' respect, if not his enthusiasm, for Pighi was shared by his wife. Pighi was a poor girl, but were they rich when they married? A poor lad loved a poor lass and God blessed them. Everything turns out right with a good heart. What good will it do them to be rich, if they don't get along? Such a temptation will take the bread from their mouths and the joy from their hearts. Besides, thank God, they had enough.

"They will be a suitable couple, Pighi and our Manolis," Reginio said, "both being so big."

"And after all it would be a pity if that Tereres married a girl like that."

"Yes, I heard that he has even asked her hand in marriage."

"And her father wants to give her to him. He is a poor man; what can he do?"

"You said it right. It is a shame."

Saitonicolis thought for a moment, then he said:

"They say that the best pear is eaten by the pig; but I won't let that tererepig eat it. The only bad thing is that Manolis is not ready to get married yet. What do you think?"

"Let's ask Pighi's father for her hand and then let a year or two pass, till the marriage takes place."

"Leave it to me; I know what to do," Saitonicolis said, as if a sudden inspiration had come to him.

And he started to go out, but Reginio stopped him.

"In truth, I forgot to tell you something."

And she related to him that two days before, while she was washing clothes at the river, the widow Zervoudhena alluded to Manolis. She paid him a world of compliments. "How handsome your son is, Reginio. The two or three times I have seen him my eyes couldn't leave him. When people are young that's the way they ought to be! But my daughter too has become quite a young lady, her name is everywhere in the city! . . . And who hasn't asked for her hand! But I want her to marry in the village so I can have her near me. She is my only child . . . ."

Saitonicolis was following his wife's account with signs of impatience, but Reginio, anticipating his refusal, hastened to say that she simply mentioned the conversation so he would know about it . . . and because her maternal vanity was flattered by the idea that her son was much sought after. But her son, of course, was not for Zervoudhena's daughter, neither was Zervodhopoula for Manolis.

"Forget that crack-brained woman!" Saitonicolis said. "I wouldn't exchange one of Pighi's fingers for ten from that line of lunatics. And do you think she is a woman? A plaything, she's still green, and whoever marries her will have to leave her in the house so that the sun will not see her and make her ill. We don't need her."

"And she is used to city life while our son is a shepherd," Reginio added.

"And when, does she say, is this wanderer coming from the city?"

"In one or two months," she says.

"Let it be; Manolis will marry Pighio. And that's that," Saitonicolis said.

The consent of Thomas, Pighi's father, could be considered certain beforehand. He was a poor man and Manolis would be an unhoped for groom, particularly preferable to Tereres. The only difficulty was that Manolis was not yet in a position to get married.

His age was not a particular hindrance, he was neither the first nor the second man to get married at his age. But he was inexperienced and needed to spend at least a year in the village before his eyes would open, so he could establish a home. Besides Saitonicolis was not in favor of prolonged engagements. They seldom come out right. Thomas was of the same opinion since he was strict to the point of eccentricity. The best thing for them would be to give their word and then they could wait for one or two years. In the meantime Manolis would acquire some experience in the world and build a house, and Pighi could prepare her dowry. Thus they would be betrothed without having the dangerous closeness of those who are engaged.

* * * * * *

Two days later, towards sunset, Saitonicolis was returning from the fields with Manolis. Both of them were holding mattocks on their shoulders; and Saitonicolis, showing his son the olive groves and orchards below the road, was telling him to whom they belonged and how much they were worth.

He showed him, among others, an extensive olive grove, and with grief told him that that property belonged to one of his uncles before '21, but now it was Turkish. Some Janissary killed his uncle and took over the olive grove. For this reason Saitonicolis "had his eye on it," hoping to recover it one day. Toward this end he had already purchased the adjacent field, in order to acquire borderland, that is the right of contiguity, and preference as a buyer.

"And if I die by then," he said, "you buy it . . . But God will give me life to ransom it on my own, as I have ransomed others.

Further down, extending their branches over the road, there were huge olive trees with trunks hollowed by age.

"These here are Frankish olive-trees. They've been standing here since the time the Venetians had Crete, two hundred years ago."

"Who were these Venetians?" Manolis asked.

"Franks."

But Manolis had no idea who the Franks were, nor was it easy for his father to make him understand, because he did not know much more either. Look, the Franks are those who live in Frankia and wear hats and tight-fitting clothes. Venetians are part of that group, too. The ruins which were still standing at the edge of the village belonged to Venetian noblemen.

What Saitonicolis knew for certain was that Crete, before it was taken by the Franks and then from the Franks by the Turks, belonged to the Christians and the Christians would take it again. And this would not be long in happening.

Now and then they were forced to get out of the way so that villagers on horseback, who went by with a greeting or a phrase, could pass. At other times they were overtaken by cows, bullocks and other animals which were excited by the goad of the hurried herdsmen or by chasing each other, and Manolis put his hoe before him to protect himself from the horns of the ill-tempered bulls. In the middle of the wide roads between the olive groves rolled waves of tramping and roaring animals and people returning from the fields. Some of the young people, riding unruly mules and holding before them bundles of hay, climbed toward the village singing.

A little later, a rounded fez appeared among the tall myrtles, which formed a fence on both sides of a side road, and approached with a dancing movement and, after a moment, Thomas showed up, a sixty-year old man with a grey moustache, whose visage had the expression of an angry wild cat. He was seated on his donkey, and his daughter Pighi followed on foot.

"Good evening, Koubare Thomas," Saitonicolis shouted to him, stopping to wait for him. "Just the man I wanted to talk to."

Thomas, formerly prosperous, had lost almost all of his wealth in unfortunate rentals of tax property, as the tax regions in which the island was divided were called. This misfortune along with age had intensified his natural roughness to the point of misanthropy. His mouth was always ready to grimace with annoyance and anger, and his smile was a rare phenomenon. The only person to whom he showed some tenderness was Pighi. But when, a few days ago, he had talked to her of Tereres as a good husband, Pighi dared tell him straight out that she did not want him, not even a picture, of him, the old man had become angry. Ah! what did she think? That they had asked for her opinion? If he decided it, the matter would be finished. He could not imagine that his daughter had made her own choice. Love for him was frivolous and immoral, and he would never permit it for his daughter. She would love only her husband, and he would choose her husband.

The father's harshness was inherited by the son, Stratis, a young man of a twenty-five, tall and well built, but of gruff disposition and peevish character.

Pighi with her inexhaustible love and patient good nature managed to disarm him of his peevishness. The tyrant, then, would smile without meaning to and think that nobody could get angry with this female.

Saitonicolis told Thomas that he wished to talk to him in private and they went ahead leaving Manolis and Pighi a few steps behind.

Alone with Pighi, Manolis found himself in the position of a man who is left unaided in the face of an unforeseen danger. The phrase which he had addressed to Pighi during the evening of the baptism now seemed to him so important, so bold, that he could not understand where he found the courage to pronounce it; and the memory of it caused him to feel so ashamed that he did not dare look at Pighi.

But Pighi also remembered that phrase and while, on one hand, she feared its possible repetition, on the other hand, she wanted to hear it again, and walked with her head bowed while her face was burning with blushes. Moreover, her excitement was heightened by the idea that Saitonicolis was talking about her to her father. She guessed as much from the glance which Manolis' father threw her, when he said to her father that he wanted to talk to him.

Manolis did not guess a thing; he was so perplexed, that he could not see very well. And he stumbled on a stone with so much force that he was compelled to jump about in a manner unsuitable to the seriousness of the occasion, in order to regain his balance.

"Virgin Mary!" Pighi called out.

Saitonicolis, hearing the fuss, turned and shouted at him:

"Watch where you're going, so you don't knock your eyes out!"

And he ran to catch up with Thomas, whose donkey, being frightened by the noise, quickened its pace.

Saitonicolis' inauspicuous phrase increased Manolis' agitation. But Pighi found an opportunity to put an end to the oppressive silence:

"Did you hurt yourself?" she asked him.

Manolis answered negatively, clicking his tongue. And then for the first time their eyes met.

Then the silence returned once again. But Pighi again found something to say:

"Where do you like it best, Manolio, in the village or in the mountains?"

"It's okay in the village," he answered.

Wanting to say something himself, he asked a silly question:

"And what about you do you like it in the village?"

But Pighi now was observing their parents preceeding them, trying to ascertain if she had correctly guessed the object of their conversation. Saitonicolis seemed to be cheerful, while Thomas was less gloomy than usual. One of the phrases of their conversation, which reached Pighi's ears, delighted her. Her father was saying: "I didn't say that Tereres is better . . . ." She did not hear anything more, but what she heard was enough to reinforce her presentiment, that at that moment Saitonicolis was saving her from the danger of becoming Tereres' wife.

Then she directed a furtive glance at Manolis and watched him with a serious and profound curiosity. Then she said to him:

"Manolio, do you want some beans!"

And stopping she presented Manolis a basket of green beans which she had hanging from her waist.

Manolis reached out his big hand to the basket, but while he bent towards the girl and his face came very near her cheek, an inebriation such as that of wine overcame him, and his hand almost changed direction. Pighi, feeling his breath burning on her face like the lava of a volcano jumped back slightly. But Manolis recovered immediately on seeing the rounded fez of Thomas, which at a short distance moved left and right like a threat.

At that moment hurried footsteps were heard and they were forced to step aside to let pass a donkey loaded with fallen branches, under whose bulk the animal, changed into a huge porcupine, was completely lost to sight. That portable forest, which barely fit on the narrow road, squeezed them as it passed and moved forward rustling noisily because of the stones which it carried along the dry dirt walls on either side of the road. Behind the donkey, Astronomos followed hastily, striking his stick against the animal's haunches crying out:

"Seeh!"

When he saw Manolis and Pighi walking together he smiled under his thick moustache and bade them good evening without stopping. Only after passing the two old men did he stop for a moment and, looking through the clearing in the trees towards the western horizon, shouted to them:

"We'll have wind. Those little red clouds are sure signs." The passing of the portable forest became an occasion of childish gaiety for the young people. When, for a moment, the branches pushed them against the wall and hid them, they laughed like children playing hide and seek; and that mirthfulness encouraged them to become more familiar.

"And what kind of work did you do today, Manolio?" Pighi asked, rearranging her kerchief, which had been snatched away by the branches.

"I was digging," Manolis answered. "Don't you see what the mattock did to my hands?"

He showed his hands, which had been blistered by the pressure of the mattock.

"And I hurt, oh, I hurt!"

Pighi comforted him. He was unaccustomed to such toil and that is why his hands were hurting, she said, but as time went by they would cease to hurt him no matter how much he would dig; they would form callouses. Needless to say, there was no derision in her phrase. And in any case, she showed him her callouses which were like "horseshoes" of hard work on her own palms.

Then Pighi related with pride that many times during the last winter when her brother was away hunting, she tilled and sowed, in order to let her aged father rest. These accounts, however, did not seem agreeable to Manolis, who wanted their conversation to take a less serious turn. But he himself did not know how to bring about such a change. That Pighi might say something to him about the phrase he addressed to her while giving her the baptismal favors, was something he feared at first; but the longer he listened to Pighi talk about other things, the more he began to wish it. He did not have the nerve to remind her of that great event. Finally, despairing, he started putting together a phrase; but when he opened his lips, his tongue became paralyzed. It would have been easier to express what he wanted to say with his hands and lips. And in truth, his movements were not restrained by shame; and at one moment, as they were passing under a dome, formed by trees spreading their thick branches over the road, while bushes on either side of them forced them to come very close, his shoulders made a movement like that of a bird of prey about to take off. But this impetus was checked by Saitonicolis' voice, summoning them to quicken their step in order to catch up with them. Their parents, it seems, had finished their private conversation and, halting, they waited for them while Manolis was obliged to swallow his phrase, as if he were swallowing a lump of quinine.

Thomas was now almost cheerful and unusually talkative. He also addressed a few words to Manolis, but while he was talking, his rounded fez caught on a branch and hung there like a bell over the road. The spectacle appeared very funny to Manolis who started laughing. Saitonicolis pulled the branch nearer with his mattock, unhung the fez and ran to give it to the old man, who being unable to stop his donkey on time, had proceeded with his head uncovered.

A little bit later a herd of animals going by separated them. Saitonicolis stayed a few steps behind with Pighi, to whom he said:

"Good luck, Pighio. I learned that you are getting married . . . with Tereres Anagnostis.

Pighi stopped walking and deathly pale looked at him; but the smile which she saw in Saitonicolis' visage restored the color of life to her face at once. She did not say anything but her big eyes filled with tears. And Saitonicolis did not want to prolong her agony.

"But tell me, don't you want Anagnostis?"

"No, Uncle Nicoli," the girl answered in the most decisive tone of voice, "I don't want him. But if my father and my brother want him, what can I do, poor me? . . . And being motherless, to whom shall I tell my grief and be comforted?"

Saying those last words, her tears began flowing.

"Don't cry, my child, don't cry," he told her affectionately, "and if you don't want Tereres, they won't make you marry him against your will. Even your father has changed his mind."

"Is that true?" Pighi cried out, not daring to believe it.

"Of course it's the truth, it's not a lie. All the time we were talking, that's what I was fighting for, to move his immovable mind. You needn't fear any more that he'll talk to you about Tereres again. Here, do you love Uncle Nicolis?"

"I always loved you like my father, Uncle Nicolis," Pighi said and started to kiss his hand; but Saitonicolis stopped her. Then, changing tone, he said to her:

"And tell me, Pighio, my child, what do you think of my Manolis?"

"What should I think of him?" she answered blushing and lowering her eyes. "Good."

"Isn't he better than Anagnostis?"

"A thousand times, a thousand," Pighi answered animatedly as her heart began to throb like a bell ringing on a festive day.

"Ah, know that your father and I have come to an agreement. I call you my child and indeed you will become my real child . . . Would I let that impotent Tereres take you? The man you'll marry will be young and strong like you and good natured like you."

But they were already entering the village and Thomas turned and called to Saitonicolis:

"Did you hear, brother Nicolis, what they are saying?"

Saitonicolis paid attention and heard the loud voice of Papadhomarkos, who from a high roof was announcing the following:

"Hey lads! all of you, Turks and Greeks, be informed that on Saturday the ditches from Mavriko to Potamissa will be cleaned, and whoever doesn't go or doesn't send a worker will pay a fine!"

Every one or two years the Moudir, in agreement with the elders, ordered that the owners of the estates adjacent to the waterways clean them by participating in a corvee, so that marshy miasmas, which impeded the flow of the waters, wouldn't develop from the accumulation of mud.

Thomas had stopped in front of the last watermill and was watering his donkey, while Papadhomarkos repeated the announcement for the third and final time. Other villagers had stopped there and were conversing about the order, raising their voices so they wouldn't be lost in the roar of the mill. All those bound to take part in the corvee complained, because one had work on Saturday which could not tolerate delay, and another found it unfair that everyone had equal obligation while the land-holdings were unequal; Saitonicolis was also bound and so he said:

I'm thinking of sending Manolis."

But Pighi intervened on behalf of Manolis.

"He is not accustomed to work and he'll get sick. Don't send him."

And Saitonicolis, smiling, bent and made her blush with a phrase:

"Have you already started caring for him?"

Then, in a loud voice so that Manolis could hear also, he said:

"As a special favor I will send a hired hand instead. Even if I must pay him five rials.[37]

Saitonicolis was so cheerful that further along, having passed the bridge over the mill-run he stopped and talked to Kartsi Nicolis, a madman, who all day would busy himself with taking water from the river in old pitchers, and then pour it on his naked feet, endlessly talking to himself.

"Good evening Nicolakis," he told him. "Won't you tell us what the plane tree is called in Turkish?"

Kartis interrupted the cold shower, which he was taking standing in front of his door, and answered:

"Kourbar-aghatzi."

"And the bush?"

"Berdheleto."

Saitonicolis laughed, although it was not the first time he heard Kartsis' improvised Turkish, or the comical song, which the latter recited after his Turkish vocabulary:

St. Stick comes down
And he has drunk some brandy .....

Thomas, however, continued serious-looking, without giving any attention. He had heard this nonsense a thousand times. Pighi, on the other hand, related frightening things to Manolis about Kartsis. It was rumored that nereids had taken away his senses; that is why many times at midnight he had been seen stark naked at the mill, where it splatters frothy water or at the water-wheel, and he was dancing with the nereids.

"And why are his hands trembling like that?" Manolis asked.

"They say he killed a wagtail. They say that whoever kills a wagtail will find his hands tremble like its tail."

When they separated, it was completely dark and Pighi, saying goodnight to Saitonicolis, quickly bent and kissed his hand.

"Listen, Manolis," Saitonicolis said to his son after supper; "tonight, I talked to Thomas on the road, and he agreed to give you Pighio. But tell me do you also want to get married?"

Manolis not only did not answer, but lowered his head, so that the happiness which flashed in his eyes wouldn't show.

"Aren't you saying anything?" Saitonicolis said to him again.

Manolis stooped even more.

Saitonicolis smiling exchanged glances with his wife.

"He must not want to get married," he said . . . "Very well, my son, I will not force you. If you don't want it, neither do I; you are the one who is going to be married, not me. Your mother told me that the day before yesterday you told her straight forwardly that you like Thomas' Pighio; but she must have seen it in a dream. She has grown old and so is forgiven. I did not give my final word to Thomas; and since you don't want the girl, I'll tell him to give her to Tereres who wants her and already asked for her."

Manolis was disturbed, but he continued to be silent.

"Shall I tell Thomas that you don't want Pighi and that he can give her to Tereres?" Saitonicolis asked again even more intensely.

The sweat of agony appeared on Manolis' forehead, as far as the blush had reached.

But his mother intervened.

"My good man, he wants her, but he is embarassed to say so. Didn't you say it to me, my son?"

Manolis put forth superhuman effort to confirm his mother's words by a slight gush of laughter.

"You rascal! You little rascal!" Saitonicolis said laughing.

5

But let us leave Manolis, who that night, in his dream, repeated a thousand times his wonderful expression of love to Pighio. At the other end of the village, we are awaited by other acquaintances and events which will have a great influence on the further development of the present story.

Kalio Zervoudhena, nicknamed Gadfly because of her tiny build and her nervous liveliness, was well preserved at an age when, usually, women villagers had become totally aged, broken by their arduous labor and the pain of motherhood.

Widowed very early, she showed intentions of righting the injustice of fate. For one reason or another she had passed forty and was nearing forty-five, without having realized her desire, but also without losing hope. This, at least, is what the fellow-villagers gathered from the coquettish attention which she always showed to her dress, particularly as her age progressed, from her attempts to conceal her real age, and from the youthful liveliness of her movements. Nobody ever saw her barefoot outdoors, like other women, even young and unmarried, who seemed to consider shoes a needless luxury.

This was enough for her to become the object of common derision and gossip, though, no matter how hard the gossips tried, they were never able to find in her conduct anything more than the flightiness which it lent to her.

When he died, her husband left her, along with the sorrows of untimely widowhood, considerable wealth and a daughter, Marouli as she was called, who had become a delicate young lady, cold and, in contrast to her mother, untalkative with the tight-lipped dignity of a young noblewoman come rain or shine. And indeed she had been raised as the noblewoman of the village, "without the sun having seen her," as her mother would say. She had not come to know the hardships of farming life, while the majority of the young girls entering adolescence and often older than that, could not be distinguished from the boys with whom they spent the day except for their attire; nor did she ever wake up on winter nights "at the hour Orion comes out" to feed the oxen, she never dug, nor did she harrow or burn under the flaming sun while harvesting and winnowing. She had just barely learned how to harvest and gather olives, and that only after taking great precautions for the protection of the delicate white of her face and her hands. Most of the time she would go into the shade, to sew or weave. As a weaver, she was peerless; likewise her embroidery was famous.

The other girls of her age admired her "nobleness and skillful handiwork" and when she went to gather greens, she was accompanied by an entire court of female admirers, who wandered for hours in the fields, singing and laughing, exchanging improvised verses finding faults in young men or their rivals, asking the daisies whether they were going to heaven or hell: "I'm going to the pitch of hell, I'm going to paradise," and asking for sentimental omens in the flight of small insects, which they released into the air.

Tell me whom shall I marry!
Tell me whom shall I marry!

Her friends, completely burned by the sun and hardened by hard work, often took her delicate hands in theirs and observed them as if they were wonderful works of art.

"My God, how white you are, Marouli!"

Some of them, though, could not bear her, some because they were jealous and others not being able to stand her haughtiness.

The widow's daughter indeed held her nose quite high, thinking that only she existed and no one else, as the others expressed it. This conceit had been nurtured by her mother's frivolity, through excessive praise. Her "pillar of perfection" had all endowments; she left nothing for anyone else. Her dowry, her manners, her dress, her way of walking, her look, everything about her was unique and a source of pride and inexhaustible chatter for Zervoudhena.

Zervoudhena loved her with the same lightheadedness and exaggeration she showed in everything, while the hyperbolic praise and endearments which she lavished on her "pillar" greatly contributed to the girl's raising her nose so high. Nevertheless, for some time, the vilifying gossips held that the daughter's advancing age had begun to disturb the mother, and that for two years now Marouli had been eighteen, so the widow could still say that she had not yet turned forty.

After a sojourn of a few months in the city with one of her uncles, she returned with new claims to pride and disdain of the villagers, male and female, from whom she was distanced not only by natural graces but also by acquired ones. Marouli returned from the city with new clothes, new manners, new language, a new name and a new nose.

The naive neighbor women, who had never been away from the village, listened with astonishment to Zervoudhena calling her daughter "Marghi." The widow explained that in the city they do not say Marouli, but Marghi; and that her daughter no longer wanted to be called by that rustic name. In truth, didn't the new name have more nobility? The widow repeated it, drawing her voice out in order to show all its music and gentility.

Then shaking her head she would say:

"What are we talking about when we say we live in this world and are doing things! You should hear her relate all the good things of the city and its luxuries and your head would spin!"

But all the wonders which she herself had not described were demonstrated by the finery with which she returned from the city: the star-covered silken gauze, which was wrapped around her blond hair, the golden cross, which was playing and glittering on her snowy neck, the pelisse, a fur vest which, opened in front, left to the imagination the divine charms of the virgin bosom beneath the gossamer blouse-front, and then the many-pleated dress with furbelows, the stockings and high heels.

But Marghi reserved her greatest surprise for the villagers for the following Sunday, when she went to church in crinoline or as it was more commonly known, *"malako."* The widow's daughter entered the church with the gait of a queen, followed by her mother, who was so swollen with pride that it was possible to assume that she too was wearing crinoline. Rustling like a machine, she passed amidst slight exclamations of surprise and admiration, and stood at the very front, no longer like a "pillar," but as a veritable tower of "Malakof."

There was so much movement and so much whispering among the women, that some of their husbands turned away, fretting. One after the other the women approached to look at that miraculous outfit and timidly reached out with their hands and touched it lightly on the surface, addressing different questions to the daughter, which the mother hurried to answer.

There was only one woman who deigned merely to turn her head towards the noise and the bulk of crinoline; a tall, beautiful and dusky lass who was standing next to the Presbytera in the place of honor before the icon-screen. This haughty one was the Captain's daughter, the only one whom Marghi recognized as a rival. The mother and daughter got the impression that Angeliki "turned yellow from her jealousy," whereas she had merely smiled. As a matter of fact, the lightheadedness of the spoiled Marghi could only rouse laughter in the masculine character of the Captain's daughter, who, having been raised among six brothers, themselves the bravest of the young men of the village, had very few female frailties. Like the virgin of the popular song:

Who had twelve brothers and eighteen male cousins.

Angeliki was proud of her "fearless" brothers and often competed with them in their games. Hence her beauty had acquired the modest and proud plasticity of an Artemis.

The other women continued to admire Zervoudhopoula's refinement; while the widow, inebriated by her impression, forgot where she was and unreined her loquaciousness. Angry "shhhs!" repeatedly came from the men's side, but the widow, interrupting her prattle for a while, would begin again even more boisterously, while her daughter tightening her thin lips, displayed herself fixed in the middle of the church as if she were an *epitaphios*.[38]

The crinoline had only a humorous effect on the men. When, after the end of the liturgy, Marouli was passing among them towards the church yard, she was greeted by small outbursts of laughter. "What is that? A dress or a basket? If someone were to put it in his garden, he would need nothing better as scarecrow for the birds." This mirthful impression was intensified by Astronomos' comment, that she needed a whole furlong in order to pass by.

Kalio had purposely lingered a while in the church, in order to find an excuse to trumpet the name, which, along with the crinoline, her daughter had brought from the city. And when she emerged, flushed and shining with pride, her eyes searched the crowd for her daughter, who had preceded her, and called out so loud that everybody could hear her:

"Marghi, hey Marghi! wait for me, my child."

And passing among the smiling villagers, who were whispering how that unfortunate gadfly had gone mad, she informed everybody left and right that "in the city they don't say Marouli, but Marghi."

At the corner of the church, Marghi, separated from the women accompanying her, surprised them anew with a previously unheard of salutation, accompanied by a regal nod of the head:

"Adio![39] . . . . Come, mother . . . ."

The villagers' laughter burst out noisily, and when Marghi turned the corner of the church and went away with her mother, Astronomos, imitating her movements and voice, repeated:

"Adio! . . . . Come, mother . . . . ."

And then, with the same drawl, he said:

"What kind of a tree does wheat bear?"[40]

From the height of her nose it was to be expected that she saw everything in the village small and base from the houses to their inhabitants. She considered no one worthy of the honor of becoming her husband. Smyrnios alone, in her opinion, stood out. He was the first among the grooms, just as she was the first among the brides. Starting with the idea that both had seen the world, she nurtured fraternal feelings for him, which tended to be transformed into love. But this preference was kept so deep in her little heart that even her mother guessed nothing.

And even after her return from the city, Marghi continued every evening to go to the fountain, where she learned the women's news of the day, what one woman said and what another did, what one woman wove and what the other unraveled. There, resting their pitchers on the cornice of the fountain and waiting their turn, women, young and old, would chatter for a while and then one by one would leave with pitchers on their shoulders.

But, as a proverb says, the pitcher goes to the fountain many times, but there is a time when it does not return. This is what happened to Marghi's pitcher. One day it went to the fountain, but it never came back. Only Marghi returned, miserable, wet from head to toe, like someone shipwrecked holding only the ornamented handle.

"What happened to you?" Kalio asked her troubled. "Did you fall down?"

"Patouchas . . . that accursed Patouchas . . . ." the lass stammered, unable because of the sobs to complete her phrase.

And her tears accentuated the spectacle of wetness, as if to present the event more tragically.

"What did Patouchas do to you?"

"He threw a stone at me . . . and broke the pitcher on my shoulder," Marghi finally managed to say.

"But why! has he gone mad?" Kalio said amazed.

"How do I know what came over that lunatic!"

But that was not the first time that Patouchas had bothered her. Marghi related how for days whenever he met her, he shot such glances at her that one would think that he wanted to swallow her. Sometimes he would say a few words to her from a distance. It seemed he was trying to show her love; that evening, wanting to imitate the other young men, who at dusk watched for the passing of the young girls returning from the fountain, Manolis bothered them by throwing small stones at their pitchers, and the clumsy oaf broke hers.

"But didn't they say that he was promised to Thomas' Pighi?"

"From the day he saw me with the crinoline he's been bedeviled!" Marghi said, wiping her tears with the edge of her apron.

Trembling all over with indignation she uttered a terrible threat:

"Just let him talk to me one more time, and if I don't grab a stone and break his head, don't call me Maria but Fatouma![41] There."

"Don't worry, daughter, don't worry, my Marghi," the widow said to her soothingly, "I'll talk to his father. Imagine the things that big fool is doing!"

And after thinking for a while she said as if talking to herself:

"But have they broken with the Thomases . . .? Strange thing! Let me tell you something, my child, he is a good young man, and if it's true that he's broken his agreement with Thomadhopoula ...."

"Be quiet, be quiet," Marghi shouted outraged, "I don't want to hear you ......!"

"He is the best young man in the village," the widow insisted.

"He is the best ox in the village. Are you trying to exasperate me?"

"Listen to what I'm telling you." Kalio said, becoming stubborn in the face of contradiction. "How do you know who is good and who is bad? He is handsome and a landowner . . . ."

"Leave me alone, for the love of God," Marghi cried out impatiently, "don't compare that insipid creature, that Saracen, with handsome men!"

"Does a Bourbas know what a date is?"[42] the widow said with the voice of experience. "Men should be strong and gallant . . ."

"Ou! gallant," Marghi again said, grimacing. "Gallant like our donkey."

"And if he isn't gallant, he will be. He is only a lad. To tell the truth you are older. He's inexperienced because he was a shepherd until recently, but he'll wake up.

"I don't listen to the words of other women whom he wouldn't even want for servants. He's from a good family. And let me tell you, my daughter, it is my wish that ...."

"That I marry him?"

"Well, if they've broken with Thomas. . . ."

"Better let the devils have him! Me, take Patouchas, and be called Patouchena, me, me . . .! Earth, open up and swallow me! Are you in your right mind telling me all this?"

"In my right mind," the widow answered with calm stubborness. "You will not find any better."

Marghi, crimson with anger, looked at her mother. A terrible word came to her lips and she swallowed it. Then she said with the same rage:

"If he is the one for me, I don't want to see my fate!"

"Think about what I've said and you'll see I'm right."

"I was right when I said that you're set on killing me tonight," Marghi said and furious she threw herself into a corner, where, taking the position of a Niobe, she began to cry anew.

The motherly heart of the widow was moved.

"But, my daughter, I did not tell you to marry him willy-nilly!"

And approaching her she spoke to her affectionately and caressed her, while Marghi pushed her away like an angry child.

"Do you think I want harm to come to you, my child? I just said a word. You don't want it? I don't want it either. The world hasn't come to an end."

"But in God's name, is a man like that for me? Am I so worthless as to have to take that laughing-stock of the whole world? Heaven and earth, better let a Turkish bullet take him instead!"

Zervoudhena did not object any more, even though inwardly she insisted on her idea.

And while Marghi repeated her threat that she would crack Manolis' head, if he continued bothering her, the widow said to herself again and again:

"But how can this be? Did they break with the Thomases?"

6

In fact, Manolis was not pleased with the way his father had arranged things. The customs and the reasons with which Saitonicolis justified the postponement of the marriage for one year and, perhaps even more than that, did not have, in his opinion, any real value. Was it really necessary for him to have his own house, since he could live happily with the girl he loved in a cave or in the open air? With Pighio, even a hayloft would seem like a palace to him. His happiness was very accommodating. But he could by no means understand why they still considered him unsuitable for marriage. They said his time had not yet arrived, without asking him, without asking the person concerned, who, according to the saying, knows what the rest of the world does not.

Still he did not say anything, but showed his discontent in the gloomy reluctance with which he performed the task Saitonicolis assigned him, gathering stones and other materials for the construction of his future home. He vented his discontent on the back of the mule, which carried the stones from the quarry. Until then, the wretched animal had been gentle and obedient, but Manolis mistreated it so badly that it became peevish and acquired to Saitonicolis' great surprise, the habit of kicking.

On rare occasions, sitting on the mule, on his way back to the quarry to pick up a new load, Manolis would be seized by tender thoughts and would attempt to sing. His song often consisted of unrelated phrases and words which served simply to complete the rhythm and carry the mode. If one were to pay particular attention, it would be possible to detect in that confusion of incoherent phrases one name repeated over and over, the name of Thomas' daughter, sometimes muffled as if murmured in a kiss, sometimes shrill, like a redhot iron flung from the forge of his chest.

Aside from the singer, that primitive song also pleased the mule, because Manolis forgot to torture him during those moments. But the suffering of the wretched animal ended only when the building began and Saitonicolis burdened his son with another job, as an apprentice to the builders, preparing the mortar and the lime.

Manolis' depression was lessened by this new job. Karpathios, the master-builder, constantly gave him reason for mirth with his amusing manner of speaking. When he became angry with Manolis' carelessness, he called him "loco." Manolis became so emboldened that he began to banter with him, imitating his pronunciation. When Karpathios called him: "Manolis! Manolis!" he answered, drawling like him:

"What's your pleasure, Master? Mortar or stones?"

Manolis also laughed when Karpathios, growing upset, would shake the trowel at his face and splash him with mortar. This gave him an agreeable pretext for running to the river to wash his face and look at women washing clothes with their dresses pulled up. The builder, a cheerful man, often sang, while working, amusing songs from his part of the country; and he especially enjoyed himself by scandalizing Manolis with a song in which a young nephew flirts with his aunt:

> Go there to the swing
> With my aunt Irene.
> I push and she pushes,
> God will it and she falls.
> Here's a place and a meadow
> Ah! auntie if only you were another!

But Sykologos, the second builder, did not condescend to jest with Manolis, the blockhead who couldn't divide hay between two donkeys. Sykologos thought highly of himself, because even if he was illiterate, he knew all of the modes of ecclesiastical music and, with the help of the prompter, chanted in church. He used to say, "If I knew how to read and write . . ." (the way Bonaparte might have said, "If I had triumphed at Waterloo . . . .!"). He chanted while building and the cheerful Karpathios, whenever the psalmody irritated him, would say to Manolis privately:

"Come, my lad, if we don't go mad, we'll be sainted for sure."

Manolis was consoled by the idea that now, at least, he could see Pighi, who remained home finishing her dowry. But he forgot to take into account the old man with the rounded fez.

One day, stealing a few moments from his work, Manolis ran to Thomas' house where he found Pighi weaving. The girl turned, radiant with joy, and welcomed him.

"Be seated," she said to him, leaving her shuttle.

Manolis remained standing next to the "workshop."

"I can't," he said sadly, "because if I tarry, Karpathios will start shouting and then he'll tell my father."

With the last word a sigh escaped his chest. This was no life, working all God's day long in the sun, without a moment's opportunity to see her.

Manolis uttered this great speech, leaning on the top of the loom; as he covered his face with his wide palm to hide his embarassment it looked like he was hiding tears.

Pighi looked at him anxiously, and choking with emotion, said: "Does your father scold you?"

"Yes, if the builder tells him that I left the building, he will become furious . . . ."

"Why, why?" the maiden said, as if she were addressing her complaint to her future father-in-law. "Can't he see you'll get sick?"

"My mother told him that too, but he won't listen," Manolis answered in an almost plaintive tone. "He says he wants me to get accustomed to work. If the house is not completed, he says . . . ."

Pighi appeared pensive; then, with a little hesitation, she said: "Shall I talk to him too? It embarrasses me but I will tell him. . . ."

Manolis jumped up, joy gleaming in his eyes.

"Yes, tell him that we don't care if the house is not finished. . . ."

Pighi gazed at him in astonishment.

"We can live on our upper floor until the house is finished," Manolis continued.

Pighi began to perceive the misunderstanding between them and she blushed.

"Let's get married," Manolis was saying with an unexpected liveliness, "and let the house get done a year from now . . . . or never."

"But I can't say such things to your father," Pighi said, lowering her head.

"And what are you going to tell him?"

"Not to press you too hard at work, just to have another worker to help you."

Manolis made a grimace of displeasure.

"Hm! that's all you're going to tell him . . . Ay, don't tell him a thing," he said with the tone of a sulking child. "I don't want you to tell him a thing. Did you think work tires me? What a job! even my ear doesn't sweat!"

Angry, he made as if to leave.

"But I can't . . . how can I tell him such things?" said Pighi sorrowfully.

"I can't tell him because he's my father and I'm ashamed. Why can't you tell him?"

Pighi kept silent, ready to cry, because she could not justify herself. And Manolis, seeing Pighi becoming more bashful, became even bolder and said:

"Why don't you tell me now that you don't want us to get married, just . . . ."

"I don't want to?"

"If you did, you would tell my father that we don't care about the house, we only want to get married. Once the marriage is performed, let him make me build even ten houses."

Pighi continued her silence.

"Do you want to tell him?" Manolis asked, after waiting a few moments for her answer.

"But I can't, I told you, I can't," Pighi answered and her tears started flowing.

Manolis wanted to act angry and leave, but he did not have that much will power and instead of going away, he approached slowly, slowly, and sat on the "plank" of the loom. Moved to tears, he wanted to tell her that he would get sick, not from his efforts, but from the impatience of his love, that he no longer could live even one moment without seeing her, that his life without her was martyrdom and the like. But when he found himself near her and felt the warmth of her body, his thoughts were thrown into confusion and everything he had to say expressed itself in a fierce, savage embrace.

The girl resisted, but found it difficult to free herself from the iron circle of his arms.

"Let me go," she was telling him, "let go I tell you . . . What you're doing is bad . . . My father will come and he'll kill me . . . Manolis, please, for your mother's sake."

She repulsed him with her strong arms, and because of the fierceness of the struggle the loom shook and creaked and was in danger of falling apart.

"Manolis, the loom will break . . . look, the thread will snap . . . Manolios, please . . . !"

But Manolis, deaf to her supplications, intoxicated and inflamed by the touch and warm aroma of female flesh, confined her, helpless now, in his arms and with a voracious kiss smothered her pleas in her mouth. But that kiss resurrected the girl's modesty with such force that she managed to slip out of the embrace of the raging adolescent and with a rapid movement she threw herself out of the loom; gasping and trembling she said to him:

"Manolis, calm down, or I'll leave you alone in the house."

And she was drawing back towards the door, in order to secure her retreat in case of another attack, when the sound of steps was heard.

"My father!" she whispered, and, setting her clothes and hair in order, she ran to the loom.

Flushed, Manolis looked about him as if looking for a place to escape.

The cough of an old man came through the windows of the house, then a long piece of wood appeared as it entered through the door, and, a moment later, Thomas' fez, which had lost some of its stiffness by rubbing against the wood, came into sight. At the same time, the voice of the old man calling his daughter was heard.

"Pighio, come help me."

Pighi hurried, but Manolis arrived first and took the piece of wood from the old man's shoulder.

Thomas answered Manolis' eagerness with a glance of unhappy surprise, which became an inquiry directed at his daughter, as if saying to her: what does he want here? Then, with a sigh of weariness he sat in a chair, took off his fez and, with his index finger wiped the sweat from his brow. Then he turned toward the young man with an inquisitorial look and said to him:

"Don't you have work today, Manolio?"

"I have," Manolis answered in a timid voice.

"And why did you leave your work and wander about? Who's helping?"

Manolis lowered his head and kept silent.

"But he hasn't been away very long," Pighi said.

"You do your work and don't sprout up where you haven't been planted!" Thomas cried out angrily. "Sit down at your loom!"

Pighi obediently sat down at the loom while Thomas continued addressing himself to Manolis:

"Listen, Manolio, my child, your duty is not to come here; don't come another time. It's not proper for you to enter a house where there is a girl all by herself.... Okay, on a holiday, when I am here or my son ... you are welcome; but on weekdays you should look to your work. Do you hear what I'm telling you?"

Manolis nodded unhappily, while Thomas sneezed, and exchanged a glance of despair with Pighi. Then, as if thrown off balance, he turned with a hesitant step towards the door, where, as a final rebuff, he received on his backside another bitter expression from the old man:

"And your father, if he learns that you are neglecting your work, will be very displeased."

And while he was passing under the window, he heard him say to Pighi.

"If I catch you by your braid . . . !"

Saitonicolis' mule was fortunate because its collaboration with Manolis had ended, otherwise that day it would have gone through the most unpleasant moments of its life. So it was not enough that, without any serious reason, they condemned him to wait for a year, and perhaps more, but they also forbade him to see the one who would be his wife? This seemed so unfair and unreasonable that he thought it was being done only to torture him. He was indignant as much with his father as with Thomas.

For a moment the idea came to him to thumb his nose at the builders and the building and take to the mountains again. However, the memory of the scene at the loom restrained him. Could he live far from Pighi any more? Besides, Tereres was there, lying in wait to steal his happiness. He also found out that, that man was speaking ill of him and that Stratis, Pighi's brother, preferred Tereres, who still had hopes, it seems, of becoming his brother-in-law.

When Manolis returned to work, he found Karpathios, the master-builder, furious and threatening that he would complain to Saitonicolis. They could not build and prepare the mortar without him. Manolis, vexed as he was, shouted at him to do anything he wanted. If he wanted he could tell God too!

Indeed, he was so flushed with fury that his face had darkened.

"My god! he has the fury of an Arab today. What happened to him?" Karpathios said to Sykologos.

He worked for hours without uttering a word. Only later, towards evening, when Pighi passed by on the way to the fountain, his melancholy seemed to dissipate; the smile which accompanied her "good-evening," lit up his gloomy face.

Pighi passed by there every day, purposely wandering from her course, whenever she went to the fountain. Also from that day onward she passed by often. Her pitcher had been transformed into a jar of the Danaids.[43]

"Pighi," aren't you going to ask us how the building is going?" the builders asked her cheerfully.

"I have eyes and I can see," Pighi answered smiling.

"You can see it all right, but is it God's will that the soul for whom we work does not even say goodmorning to us?"

Manolis, roused by the appearances of Pighi, performed feats of strength, lifting like a Titan heavy corner-stones and giving them to the builders, much to Karpathios' astonishment.

"He's his mother's son, he's a regular Digenes!"[44]

Henceforth, he would call Manolis "loco" but without drawing out the word, and more guardedly.

The master-builder's admiration encouraged Manolis to attempt a different kind of feat. One day seeing Tereres approach, he said to Karpathios:

"Boss, shall I grab Tereres for you and throw him in the river, like a mouse?"

Karpathios tried to dissuade him, but Sykologos encouraged him by nodding.

Manolis needed no prompting. A wonderful idea came to him, how to punish Tereres and at the same time humiliate him in front of Pighi. The river was a few steps away, and Manolis knew that at that hour Pighi was doing laundry at the river.

The whole thing seemed extremely easy to him. Was his lean adversary in love any heavier than the granite stones which he lifted up with so much ease? But when Tereres came near and Manolis ran towards him menacingly, an unexpected difficulty arose. Tereres, stopping, drew a dagger from his sash and, trembling, said to him: "What do you want, man? Do you want me to kill you?"

Manolis' brave charge was cut short, and he too stepped back a bit. But Tereres, a prudent man, confined himself to defense, and Manolis' retreat gave the builders time to intervene.

"Okay," Manolis said then, "I'll show you another time who I really am. . . ."

"As you wish," Tereres answered.

Then, he said, mockingly shaking his head:

"Well, he's become a man and he makes threats too! May misfortune be your lot, you big ox!"

Then Manolis attempted to rush him, but the builders restrained him, while Karpathios called to Tereres:

"Go away in peace. Don't stand here making trouble!"

Tereres responded to Manolis' new threat with another provocation, this time in verse:

> Before the enemy throng he acts ready to fight
> Who meeting a single foe eye to eye shivers with fright.

And then he went away. Meanwhile, Manolis managed to put his courage together once more. Suddenly, at the moment the builders were about to begin laughing at his cowardice he pushed them away and, grabbing a shovel, dashed after Tereres. He caught up with him in front of his home.

"Hold on, you cripple," he shouted, "and draw that knife again!"

But Tereres just managed to enter his house and shut the door, which received a terrible blow from Manolis.

"Why did you lock yourself up, you old wreck, you coward?" he shouted while kicking the door in a frenzy. "Do you think I can't break down the door?"

"Go to the devil, Patouchas, or do you want me to send you to him?"

Then Manolis turned and saw something which chilled his warlike fervour. The barrel of a "kariofili"[45] had appeared through a small window and was aimed straight at him. He was forced to retreat while Tereres shouted at him from behind the window:

"Where are you going? Aren't you going to break down my door? Ftou, Patouchas, Ftou!"

Only when he was safe in a corner did Manolis turn his head and answer:

"If you have the courage, Tereres, c'mon out without a rifle!"

"Ftou!" was Tereres' answer.

"Okay, I'll find you without a rifle."

"Ftou, Patouchas, Ftou!"

And this insult, drawn out like the hissing of a snake, followed the young man as he went away.

Manolis retreated from the second attack with two opposing sentiments: the pride of a youth who for the first time has discovered in his courage that he is a man, and the humiliation of a man who hears himself insulted and provoked without being able to shut the mouth of one who curses him. It was also the first time he heard the mocking nickname they had attached to him. He could not understand its meaning very well, and it was exactly for this reason that it seemed even more humiliating.

The noise of the altercation attracted some of the neighbors and passers by. Fortunately, however, due to the noise of the water and the nearby mill, the women at the river did not hear anything. Otherwise they would have come running too. Knowing that Pighi had not heard Tereres' insults, Manolis was able to think more clearly and remember the Moudir, the gendarmes and prison. As soon as it occurred to him, he rejected the idea of running to get his father's rifle in order to lay regular seige to Tereres' house. Anyway, in the final analysis, he could not be considered defeated because he forced the enemy to close himself in his fortress.

When a little later he went to the river, he found Zervoudhena instead of Pighi. She began asking him if he had seen her daughter, and, in particular, if he had seen her in the crinoline. Did another girl in the village have her beauty and nobility?

Manolis, who in the meanwhile had discovered Pighi on a roof opposite him hanging some clothes which she had whitened in the river, barely heard the widow's chatter. But, bending over the washing place and continuing her wash, she kept on talking to him about her daughter.

She regretted that she had not left her in the city. Who was there for her to marry in the village? Nobody was really suitable for her, while in the city many noble young men were asking for her.

At the same time the widow was furtively spying on Pighi, who had a massive folded cloth on her head and stepping backwards, was unfolding it little by little on the roof to dry.

"Tell me, Manolio," the widow said to him abruptly, "is it true you were promised to Pighio?"

"How do I know?" Manolis answered.

"Then who would know? It must be a secret . . . It's true, Pighi is a nice girl, but I can't understand why your father rushed into giving his word."

"Why let Tereres marry her?" Manolis said naively.

"Ah, and if somebody else got her, you wouldn't have to fear not finding another. I tell you could have found a better one. Are you comparing yourself with Tereres? Manolios, you are the best young man of the village, and it is fitting that you marry a better girl. Do you think that if you had asked for mine that I would have said no? But why am I talking to you now since that fine-feathered father of yours was in such a big hurry? There's a saying that a good man rarely makes a mistake but when he does, it's a whopper."

Manolis would have had the patience to listen to Gadfly's chatter for hours, just to look at Pighi across the way smiling at him under the shade of the unfurled fabric. But Karpathios recalled him to his wearisome task.

In moments like these he thought those responsible for his misery were the builders. If builders did not exist, his father wouldn't build a home for him, then there would be no reason for his marriage to be postponed.

The smiles which Pighi sent him from afar, as she passed by or washed clothes in the river, were scanty sustenance for Manolis' great appetite. Pighi rarely stayed at home alone; one of the two dragons almost always happened to be there, either the old man with the rounded fez or the young man with the gloomy face. Manolis no longer dared enter without making sure that Pighi was alone. Whenever he hung around below the window, he always heard Thomas' or Stratis' voice and would leave in sorrow or cursing.

In order to allay his sorrow he found excuses to go to the river twenty times a day, where he was sure to see women washing, with their dresses drawn up. In effect, the pounding of the paddles notified him they were there. When he heard pounding, he sprang up like a war horse at the sound of a trumpet.

His preference for Pighi was still not so absolute and final as to exclude all other women from his heart. To him Pighi was really an anonymous female. He preferred her because he found her handy. Loving her, he loved Woman, so he saw Pighi's face in the face of every young and pretty woman. In his veins coursed the magic potion given to Faust, with the result that "every woman appeared to him to be as beautiful as Helen."

In these moments of "infidelity" Manolis was assisted by Pighi, without her knowing it, because she had persuaded Saitonicolis to get a worker to help him. Having more free time, Manolis extended the radius of his activity. He made friends with the young men of the village; he appeared on the roofs of houses in the late afternoon, when the girls went to the fountain or when they returned from the pastures and from time to time he would tease them in imitation of the other young men.

He was so pleased with this new phase of his life that he almost forgot Tereres. The latter also helped him in this by avoiding meeting him.

But one Sunday Astronomos met him in the street and, smiling, said to him:

"Say 'abracadabra,' Manolis!"

"Abracadabra."

"Tereres wants to grab ya."

"Manolis blushed.

"I'm looking for him too," he said, "but he is scared and hides."

"Let me tell you," Astronomos said pretending to be serious, "don't ignore this thing. Tereres is evil."

I'm not scared of him."

"You're not afraid to meet him hand to hand, but he is a magician. Do you know that?"

"Hah, and if he is a magician, what can he do to me?"

Astronomos lowered his voice and said, in a mysterious manner:

"He'll bind you!⁴⁶

Astonished, Manolis looked at Astronomos:

"Bind me!"

"Yes, he'll bind you."

Manolis laughed.

"And do you think I'll just sit and watch?"

The wily Astronomos avoided clarifying the subject; he only said:

"He won't let anybody else take Pighio from him so easily. Whatever he can do, he will."

Manolis then realized why his father, as well as others, called Astronomos "batty." Only a crazy person would believe that broken down Tereres was capable of binding Manolis. If he caught him sleeping, maybe.

Thinking these thoughts, he arrived home and was ready to repeat Astronomos' words to his father so he could laugh, when his mother came from outside and, with a worried look, said.

"What's wrong with you?" Saitonicolis asked her.

"Didn't you hear?" Reginio said, "that bewitched Tereres is making threats and says that if Manolis married Pighio . . . ."

"What's he going to do?"

Reginio hesitated to say anything.

"How do I know? . . . He'll bind him, he says."

"That's what that crackpot Astronomos told me," Manolis said laughing.

"And Zervoudhena met me on the road and told me she heard it too," Reginio added.

"She's asking for it!" Saitonicolis shouted angrily. "She hears everything and she is in on everything , that Gadfly."

"Why are you insulting the poor soul?" Reginio said.

"Because what she told you is a lie."

"She is not the only one who told me . . . ."

"No matter how many said it, it's a lie," Saitonicolis insisted, "and let's put an end to this talk . . . And if finally Tereres did say it, let him say it. Let's see, can he do it?"

"Am I a lamb that he can bind me, hand and foot?" Manolis observed.

"You be quiet!" Saitonicolis said to him sternly. "It's your fault because you let him get the upper hand. It's a pity, with your size!"

Manolis frowned.

"But what's this you're telling me," Reginio said, "that he can't do it? It's his art. Isn't he a magician?"

"Let him go to the devil; he can't do anything to me. I'm not a nobody in this town. Do you understand? And I don't want to hear any more of this kind of talk.

Reginio kept silent but her fears did not subside completely. Zervoudhena had deeply frightened her. According to what the widow had heard, Tereres was threatening not only that he would bind Manolis if the engagement with Pighio took place, but that he would also load the bindings in his rifle and shoot Manolis with them so his rival would remain bound for life.

Manolis also began to worry, especially when he saw that his parents avoided giving him a clear explanation in response to his questions. On one hand, it was impossible for him to imagine being bound without rope, and he had sufficient confidence in his strength not to fear humiliation, but on the other hand, the involvement of witchcraft enveloped Tereres' menace with a mysterious power. As a magician, Tereres was no longer alone but accompanied by demons.

Having been silent a while, Saitonicolis flared up again. Addressing his son, he said:

"It's not Tereres' fault, it's yours, you lummox, for letting him defy you when you quarrelled. Do you think that I didn't find out? You gave him the courage to even threaten us. What did God give you those big hands for?"

"Well, he didn't stand still. He went and locked himself in his house," Manolis said blushing.

"You should have cracked his skull when he was threatening you before he locked himself up. You didn't act right. I forgive you since it's your first time . . . But I want to say that, since then, it seems that Tereres has put a bold face on and has began to menace us too."

Manolis had gotten up. Grabbing his gnarled stick, he rushed outside. His worried mother hurried to the door.

"Son, where are you going? For God's sake, don't do anything foolish."

"I'm not going anywhere," Manolis said, without turning his head and moved along quickly, kicking the stones on the road.

"Let him go," Saitonicolis said, pushing his wife from the door.

Popping his head out, he called to his son in the distance.

"If you find him, give it to him and don't be scared."

And because his wife grumbled and nearly cried from anxiety, he told her to mind her distaff. It was none of her business. Would she rather that Tereres lead him around by the nose? He knew what he was doing and he had no need of her opinion.

Then he threw himself in a chair, looking exhausted as if he had been digging for hours.

As Manolis was rushing off he was planning terrible things, the least of which was to kill Tereres. To tear him in two, to cut him into pieces. Looking at his gnarled oak stick, he murmured:

"A blow on the head with this should be enough for him -- he won't have the time to even say ah!"

But, little by little, his thoughts began to cool down and his wrath subsided like mercury in a thermometer. Tereres the man did not scare him exactly but Tereres the magician bothered him. Of course, he had no precise idea of the malignant power of a magician, but it was precisely this vagueness that magnified even more the idea of his opponent's supernatural aid, and his worries increased accordingly. For this reason, after a while, he lowered his sights from the head to the neck. And he thought:

"It's best to seize him by the neck and choke him like a chick. Didn't my father ask what these hands are good for?"

Then his plans reached the back:

"It would be better if I beat him like a donkey."

At the same time a dark problem kept turning around in his mind: what was that binding Tereres threatened him with? The road took him past Thomas' house. When he looked up and saw the basil and the carnations on the window, he forgot all about Tereres and his tragic decisions. Instead of getting on with the search for his enemy, he directed himself at the door before him. This decision was not entirely unrelated to the reason why he rushed out with so much force a while ago.

Pighi was there, but unfortunately not alone.

Stratis, standing next to the jug stand, was cleaning his rifle, and his sister, bent before the fireplace, was lighting a fire.

When he saw Stratis, Manolis hesitated for a moment and almost started to go back. And although Thomas had told him that he could call on them on holidays, he felt it necessary to justify his visit and said that he came to ask for his mother, whom he thought he would find there.

"Isn't my mother here?" he asked.

"No, she didn't pass by here," Stratis said, almost without turning towards the visitor.

Then he muttered a single word: "Enter." He did not interrupt his work, but turning the barrel down he poured the black rinsings into the sink. But Pighi had gotten up and offered Manolis a seat.

"Welcome, Manolis . . . be seated."

"But I was thinking of going further . . . ." Manolis said, but instead of going further he came in and, with a feigned unwillingness, sat down.

Pighi again turned towards the fireplace and continued blowing to get the fire going. And Stratis, continuing to clean his rifle, told Manolis how he had found traces of a hare and so that evening he would lie in wait by the light of the moon. This peevish, laconic young man became talkative and his harshness softened only when he talked about his passion for hunting. Even now, relating his different hunting experiences, he appeared to forget his dislike for Saitonicolis' son, and his face took on an almost kind expression.

In the meantime, they could hear the noise of children running on the roof and shouting: "Round n' round the threshing floor." Manolis, who was sitting directly under the skylight in the roof, turned his head upwards at intervals and watched anxiously because it was likely that those devil children would throw a stone at his head.

The wood in the fireplace, instead of flames, gave off smoke. Choking, Pighi was forced at intervals to draw back with tearful eyes. But, in the meantime she tossed a clandestine smile to Manolis.

Stratis, seeing Manolis watch the sky-light, took the opportunity to say that in Lasithi[47] they place half of a hollow tree-trunk, called a *roroski,* against the chimney flue; thus the wind is held back while the smoke goes out. Stratis was world-travelled; he had travelled as far as Lasithi and with a sort of conceit he flaunted his superiority. And he related various curiosities about that mountainous district, dwelling heavily on hunting. In the winter the people of Lasithi, he was saying, rarely hunt hares with rifles. They capture them in the snow, where their easily discernible tracks lead the hunter straight to their hiding place. But the snow must be fresh so that the tracks will be distinct and not covered up. It is true that the hare takes care to confuse his pursuers, and when he arrives at the place where he wishes to hide, he interrupts his tracks with a big jump and hides beneath a bush where the snow almost covers him entirely. Even if he hides his body, he cannot manage to hide his breath which filters through the snowy bush like light smoke. Guided by this, the hunter approaches and kills the hare with a club. But who cares? Hunting without a rifle is not real hunting. It is like gathering greens.

Manolis, however, heard very little of Stratis' account because his attention was interrupted either by the children making noise on the roof or by the view out the opposite window where nearby Mount

Kavalaras rose straight up into the sky. Indeed, at its peak, one could make out Derne's home. He was a Turk who especially impressed Manolis because of the cone-shaped shell which he wore on his head as an indication of some religious status related to circumcision. Lower down, at the foot of the mountain, a Turk could be seen cutting a plane-tree; Manolis would watch the ax fall and after a few seconds he would hear the hollow blow. Then Tereres and the obscure problem of the binding again came to his mind. What's this binding all about?

A shadow which had fallen on his shoulder along with a small rock, interrupted the order of his thoughts and forced him to turn up to the opening in the skylight in which he saw the cunning face of a child who was whispering:

"Patouchas . . . Patouchas!"

Manolis was upset and made a secret, threatening sign to the child who withdrew but appeared once again and whispered to Manolis through the opening:

"Patouchas . . . Patouchas!"

Fortunately these unpleasant whispers were lost in the noise of a shot, because Stratis, finishing his rifle cleaning burned it out.

Manolis was afraid that even if Stratis had not, perhaps Pighi had heard something. When the child's face appeared again in the skylight, he bit his forefinger[48] and fired such a threat with his glance that the child did not dare repeat the insult. At the same time Manolis lifted up his head in an effort to be heard by the little brat, but not by Stratis and Pighi, and whispered:

"I'll give you to old man devil, you little shit!"

In order to find some sort of diversion from his agitation, he said to Stratis:

"When I came, I was so agitated I couldn't see past the end of my nose."

"How come?" answered Stratis who at that moment was placing his rifle on the wall.

Pighi simultaneously turned from the fireplace.

"That Tereres annoys me . . . ."

Upon hearing Tereres' name, Stratis' face assumed to its previous harshness.

Pighi got up and, resting her hands on the pitchers, appeared to be watching the pot or the fire, but all her attention was directed to Manolis.

"Do you know what he's going around saying in the village?"

Manolis continued. "That he's going to bind me, he says . . . if I marry Pighio . . . "

Pighi sat down again and started stirring the fire feverishly. It was with difficulty that Stratis, watching Manolis, restrained himself from saying something offensive!

"Have you gone crazy?" he said, finally.

"But what in the devil is this binding he's going to do to me? I don't understand," Manolis insisted. "Do you yourself understand, Stratio?"

Stratis jumped up.

"What kind of words are you using!" he shouted. "If you don't understand, don't talk!"

"What did I say?" Manolis said astonished. "Do you think I'm lying to you? If you don't believe me ask my mother . . . Tereres is threatening he will bind me."

"Shut up, you devil, I say shut up!" Stratis shouted in a frenzy. "You don't say things like that in front of women."

Manolis' eyes turned from Stratis to Pighi in desperation and astonishment.

He again tried to say something, but Stratis did not give him a chance. He took him by the arm and said to him:

"Let's go outside and I'll tell you. . . ."

In good faith, Manolis followed him. So great was his agitation that he did not even turn towards Pighi, who was watching them, equally surprised, but more worried. Her brother's wrath seemed inexplicable to her, too, and she ascribed it to his preference for Tereres and his aversion to Manolis.

"Let me tell you, Manolis," Stratis said to his future brother-in-law in a tone which showed very little congeniality, when they had gone a few steps from the house, "I wanted to tell you not to get my sister's name mixed up with your fights and your spittle. But now, since you've given me an opportunity, I'm telling you once and for all; don't let my sister's name escape your lips and don't set foot in our house again."

"Come on now, I'm not going to hurt your sister!" Manolis said with a gesture of indignation.

"Listen to what I'm telling you!" Stratis said trembling in anger. "When my father has given her to you, take her and keep her. But before you marry her, don't come into our home . . . because as God is my witness . . ."

He was not through with the threat, but it wasn't difficult for

Manolis to guess it and with a grand gesture of indifference, he answered:

"I'm not going to wear black."[49]

And he went away.

"Let your keepers teach you how to talk first and then go into other people's homes," Stratis said. "It's not your fault, but my crack-brained father's."

"If you see me again in your house, spit on me!" Manolis said turning around. "Do you hear? Spit on me!"

And he went on walking aimlessly, but rapidly. It was impossible for him to understand anything of what happened. He was particularly incapable of understanding what kind of people they were, this father and son. They were incomprehensible, possessed people. They wanted to make him a son-in-law and then they treated him like an enemy. They invited him to their home and then they sent him away. The father wanted him, the son hated him. And in front of his sister, Stratis harassed him in the most barbarous manner. He started talking about Tereres and he took Tereres' side and became angry with him . . ." So! Did he say he didn't want him to go to their home? Very well, he would never go again. Stratis did not want him to talk to his sister? He would not talk to her. Let them boil her. Thank God, there were other, better girls in the village.

The thought of revenge calmed him a bit. Moreover, he realized that Pighi was the source of all his unhappiness. It was because of her that he was at odds with Tereres. It was because of her that they had given him a nickname and even the children called him Patouchas. He decided not to see Pighi again and he kept to his decision. He stopped passing by the Thomas's house. At dusk, instead of hanging around to see Pighi on her way to the fountain as he did before, he appeared on the rooftop with a colorful scarf on his shoulder. With other young men he would watch the girls returning from their tasks in the fields.

During these moments Manolis' eyes sparkled like the fuse of a bomb ready to explode with foolishness. Fear prevented explosion of his passion and he seldom even dared address a flirtatious word to the girls passing by. Gradually, however, his youthful vitality prevailed, leading him astray and into bold actions. One such moment had resulted in the widow's daughter returning home with a broken pitcher.

At first Saitonicolis saw his son's growing boldness with satisfaction. And, as they say, his heart became a garden, when during holidays he saw his son conversing affably or playfully scrapping with young men on the rooftops. But when, one after another, accusations began to come from various villagers that his son had bothered one man's daughter at the fountain, that he flirted with another in the fields and fathers and brothers threatened that they would beat him up, his satisfaction changed to worry. When, later on, he learned what happened between Stratis and Manolis, he understood why his son had gone astray. He turned to Thomas and complained to him about Stratis' conduct. Stratis should not forget Manolis lack of experience and instead of blowing up at him, he should guide and advise him. Thomas refused to listen; on the contrary, he commended his son.

"He told him the right thing . . . . If I was in his place I would've told him the same thing . . . . Let me tell you, Koubare Nicolis, it's an honor and a pleasure for me to have our families are to be related by marriage. God knows how happy I was when you said we should become relatives. Because it's true I won't find more honest or better relatives than you and your family. But I like things to be neat and orderly. I'm a poor man, but I regard my honor and reputation higher than anyone else. And I don't want anyone to prove me wrong. Do you want my daughter to marry your son? If you want it once, I want it a thousand times. We gave our word. I will wait till you are ready. But, in the meantime, I don't want you son coming into my house, because I would rather die than have my daughter's reputation ruined. A promise can be made and broken . . . And you yourself, Koubare Nicolis, if you, as well as any other honorable man, were in my place, you would do the same thing. If again you regret what you've done, that's fine with me. You can take back your word but we'll still be friends."

Saitonicolis recognized the fact that Thomas was basically right and saw that Manolis' only salvation was for the marriage to take place as soon as possible. But the house was not finished yet and the coming winter would slow construction even more. More important, however, was the fact the Manolis was still unfit for marriage.

At the same time he did not judge his son's misconduct too severely. Youth without liveliness is inconceivable; it is not youthe. He was a young man and his blood boiled. If young people do not behave recklessly, who will? The old people? After all, were not the scatterbrained antics of youth the best part of life? For this reason he hesitated. He did not want Manolis to experience the tribulations of life so soon without letting him enjoy his youth for one or two years. The only problem was that Manolis, lacking experience and being excessively impetuous, seemed to lose control and go beyond what was proper in his youthful rashness.

Saitonicolis was struggling with this perplexing problem when Zervoudhena reported to him, with all the tragic exclamations of the language, the incident with her daughter and the pitcher. Saitonicolis laughed unintentionally and this inflamed the widow even more. She told him to control his son, because, even if she did not have a husband, she was capable herself of sending him home some day with his skull cracked. Since they had promised him to Thomas' daughter, what did he want with her daughter? Unless, of course, they had broken off. Then . . . that would be a different matter.

With the last phrase her anger abated somewhat and she continued in a more restrained manner:

"I like Manolio, I told you once before, and I'd be pleased to have him as my son-in-law. In my opinion, he's the best young man in our village and let those who are jealous say whatever they like. He's a bit immature, but as time goes by he'll learn and he'll live happily with his wife as you have with Reginio. Like father, like son, isn't that what they say? But by your word, you hurried to shake hands with Thomas as if time was running out . . . They're right when they say that a good man seldom makes a mistake, but when he does, it's a whopper. Aren't there any other girls in the village?"

And she would have made some rather unpleasant comparisons for Pighi, that is if she had not been restrained by Saitonicolis' angry frown.

Thus she limited herself to saying:

"Pighi is a good girl. I won't say she isn't. But the village has others a hundred times better."

"Good or bad, she's the one he's marrying." Saitonicolis said heatedly. "I don't give my word twice. I like Pighi and what one likes is best in the world for him."

"Yes, but let's see what Manolis says about it. You like her but is he happy that he's going to marry her?"

"Like her or not, he's going to marry her!" Saitonicolis said, his temper flaring up. "Who gives the orders here, him or me? And who told you he doesn't like her? He likes her and he likes her a lot."

"If he likes her, why is he drooling over and bothering other people's daughters?" Kalio said, flaring up in turn.

"I am telling you that he'll marry the girl I want, and that's all there is to say about it."

"I'm not saying he shouldn't marry her. What do I care? Let him marry whomever he wants, in health and with pleasure, but I don't want him bothering my daughter again."

"He won't bother her any more. I don't like this nonsense either and I'm going to pull in his reins."

"You'll be doing the right thing, because he's going to get himself in trouble."

That evening Saitonicolis went home resolved to reprimand Manolis quite harshly. Until now, he had gotten along well with all the villagers. They all respected and deferred to him. Now his handsome son's foolishness would make the whole village rise against him. He wanted his son to enjoy himself as a young man. Manolis could play and laugh with the other young men, but he should love one girl virtuously and honorably. He should not stand open-mouthed whenever he saw a spoon and bother one girl and then another. Someone could end up killing him and he would die for nothing.

Entering the house, he gruffly asked his wife who was busy serving dinner:

"Isn't what's his name here yet?"

"Who's what's his name?" Reginio said, turning around.

"Manolios."

"And why do you call him that?"

"Wouldn't I be right to call him a donkey too with all his jackassed behavior? He'll get me in trouble with the whole world. Didn't you see what he did again last night? He's been bothering Marouli, Zervoudhena's daughter for a few days now. Late last afternoon, when she was returning from the fountain, he threw a stone and broke her pitcher. Do you hear what that nut is doing? And it's not only that, it's a shame for a young man who is promised to another to bother other girls. He'll get into trouble too. Somebody might kill him because nobody wants his sister or daughter to be bothered."

"Christ, protect my child . . . ! Saitonicolina said.

She was interrupted by the entrance of Manolis, who had a colorful scarf on his shoulder and a sprig of basil on his ear. But when he saw his father, he quickly removed the basil from his ear. He became serious and sat in a dimly-lighted place, according to his past custom.

"Where were you wandering around at this hour?" Saitonicolis said to him.

"Where did you see me wandering?" Manolis said, with this displeasure of one being wronged. "The builders were quite late. Then I went to the river, to wash and I came straight home."

"Do you want me to believe that? Where were you going when I was coming home? Why don't you tell me where you found the basil you had on your ear? Did you pick it up at the river or did it grow on the wheel-barrow? Come, let's have supper and then I'll show you how many pears you can pack in a sack."[50]

But his wrath evaporated little by little, and the rest was extinguished by the wine with which he washed down his dinner. By the time the table had been cleared, and he turned to his son to scold him, his face belied the hardness of his voice.

"Tell me, you sluggard, what are you doing? You seem to have decided to try every harebrained escapade in the world."

"What harebrained things did I do?" responded Manolis with unexpected composure.

"Do you have the gall to ask? When you baptized Koubaros Moustovasilis' daughter, didn't you tell your mother that you wanted Pighi . . .? Didn't he tell you, Reginio?"

"He certainly did." Saitonicolina answered with a smile.

"Then I also asked you and you didn't say no, and because I like Pighi too, I gave my word to Thomas. Won't you tell me now what's gotten into you? Why have you deserted Pighi? Why are you chasing after other girls, now one and then another?"

"What do you want me to do, close my eyes and not look at girls?" Manolis said with a smile, but without raising his eyes.

That smile impressed Saitonicolina as being impudent.

"When I talk to you," he shouted, "don't laugh. Look at that jackass! You better shut them, do you hear? You must shut your eyes. An honorable man loves one woman. He doesn't love a thousand."

Saitonicolis' anger might not have stopped there, but might quite possibly have ended with a slap on Manolis' face, if one of his beloved anecdotes hadn't come to mind as a soothing distraction to end his wrath, as Athena put an end to the wrath of Achilles when he was about to draw his sword.

"You're going to be like that other fellow," he said, almost smiling. "His father told him to marry, but he didn't want just one woman but insisted on ten. 'Come on, son, come to your senses.' He

98

stuck to his guns: 'I want ten, I said.' After trying several times and realizing that he couldn't bring him to his senses, the father pretended to agree. 'Fine, you want ten women? Marry them, my son, I don't want to make you unhappy. Since the law doesn't permit Christians to marry several women at the same time, marry one now, and every ten or fifteen days marry another. Within a year you'll have married them all. The son kept his word and married one of them. And, after fifteen or twenty days had passed, his father went and found him. He was sitting in the sun with his ears drooping like a tired donkey. 'Hey! how're you doing' he says to him, 'it's time that I got you another woman.' 'I don't want another one. What for? This woman I've married is enough for me, more than enough.' 'But you wanted ten . . . .' 'No, no, I don't want another.''

Manolis laughed, but he laughed at that young man's foolishness for not insisting on the other nine women.

"You must be in the grips of such a madness too,'' Saitonicolis continued. ''You think one isn't enough and have decided to go after whomever you see. You're a lucky fellow, but have a little patience while your house is built and your brains set. Then, when you marry Pighi, you'll come and tell me she's not only enough for you, but that she's more than you need.''

Saitonicolis was laughing, but Manolis had become very serious. In a calm and decisive voice, he flung the following announcement at his father.

''I'm not going to marry Pighi!''

His parents exchanged a glance which meant ''Haven't I told you so?''

''You aren't going to marry her?'' Saitonicolis asked in a half-choked voice.

Manolis had leaned over and was scraping the mud off his shoes.

''And why not, if we may ask such a question?''

''Because those Thomases are not human,'' Manolis answered with indignant gestures. I haven't heard a single kind word from their mouths. When they see me enter their house, they turn into devils. A few days ago I went to tell Stratis about Tereres and his threats to bind me. Before I could finish, he exploded at me and began shouting and acting enraged: 'Get out of our house, don't come into our house again and let those who own you teach you how to talk.' So I told him I wouldn't go into their house again, never in a hundred years, and I left. If I go there again, I'll have to crawl on all fours, like a pig. Let them bawl out their daughter. Another time the old man insulted me so much I couldn't see where the door was . . . . I don't want to know them any more. Let them keep Pighio. I wouldn't want her even if they covered her with gold."

Manolis' speech touched his father and if he had been one of those men who go back on their word and if he had not known that Pighi was as blameless for the rudeness of her brother as she was for the excessive strictness of her father, he would perhaps, have told him "Very well, my son, you are right. I agree the marriage shouldn't take place." Nevertheless, he considered his promise inviolable, especially since he was responsible for the rejection of another man's proposal to Pighi. In addition, he recognized that the Thomases were, at least partially, justified in their position.

"You're right, my son, but so are they," he said gently. "You enter their house with good and honourable intentions, but people are cruel and they talk. If our agreement is broken, the girl will be ruined. That's why Thomas told you not to go into their house when Pighi is alone. But Stratis was wrong in becoming angry and insulting you because you said something you didn't know was wrong."

"I didn't tell him anything bad, for God's sake! On my soul!" Manolis said heatedly.

"You told him that Tereres is threatening to bind you and you asked him what this binding meant. One doesn't say such things in front of girls. But let it be, the world hasn't come to an end. He could have talked to you nicely, like a civilized person. But you know he is hot-tempered and contrary."

"Why don't you say the other reason too?" Saitonicolina said. "You see, son, Stratis wanted Tereres as a brother-in-law and that's why he's doing these things."

"Birds of a feather flock together," Saitonicolis added. "But poor Thomas has a kind heart. Don't pay attention to his peevishness and his grumbling. Suffering has made him this way. In the last analysis, you're not going to marry Thomas nor Stratis. It's Pighi you're going to marry. She's pure gold, poor soul, and you're going to live in your home without troubles and without discord."

"And let's not forget. Aren't you doing him a favor, my son," Reginio said, "by deserting Pighi so he can give her to Tereres? If you don't give in to his spite, you'll drive him wild."

As the sparkle in his eyes indicated, this argument had more effect on Manolis' mind than all of Saitonicolis' lengthy advice. In the meantime, however, the significance of Tereres' threat had not stopped torturing his thoughts. What was this binding anyway, and why did they avoid giving him a clear explanation, and why did they tell him that he was wrong to mention it in Pighi's presence? He had begun to be possessed by mysterious worries, and imagined Tereres contriving infernal machinations against him.

In any case, because he conceived of the binding literally, he only wondered about the manner in which it would be done. At the same time, he was planning some similar revenge himself. It is certain that Tereres had already begun to inspire a paradoxical and inexplicable fear in him, even though he had the conviction that with one punch he could crush that weakling. Several times, after his heroic expedition which ended at Thomas' home and in his dispute with Stratis, he met Tereres, but he dared not carry out his resolution. The magician's eyes provoked an incomprehensible timidity in him.

"Then," Saitonicolina continued, "don't you feel sorry for poor Pighi? That barbarian Stratis took it all out on her that day and, since then, the poor soul has been crying inconsolably because her brother insulted you. I go every day to see her and I always find her with tears in her eyes. She's always asking me what she's done to you, if her brother is to blame and why you don't pass by their house any more so at least she can hear your steps and see you from a distance. She chances to see you once or twice on the way to the fountain or church, but you pretend not to see her and her heart breaks. Only God knows her sorrow, but what can she do? What can she say? She says she wants you to come to their home and that she's not afraid of anything, because a clear sky has no fear of lightning. But can she go against the will of her father and brother?"

His mother's words aroused in Manolis a feeling mixed with compassion and selfish joy. He felt sorry and he was proud, imagining those beautiful eyes crying for his sake. And Saitonicolis, guessing the effect of his wife's words, reinforced them with a couplet:

D'you see, silly bird, what you've wrought
Spurning the basil and thinking impetuous thoughts.

"Spurning Pighi," he continued, "and chasing one girl after the other. By God above, together they aren't worth her little finger! What can I do for you? I am not your age so you could see how to choose a girl. Ay, Reginio . . .? We must be careful," he said laughing, "so you don't become jealous."

"I'm so frightened!" Saitonicolina said, laughing.

Saitonicolis' cheerfulness was such that he began to slowly sing an old song:

If I were young, single, rich and brave.

Manolis was turning around and, without meaning to, in his confusion used his knife to carve on the chair on which he was sitting.

"Let it be," Saitonicolis continued, "I understand that whatever bad things your lips may say about Pighi, your heart doesn't mean it."

"I don't want her, I don't want her, I say!" Manolis said, gathering his defeated stubborness for the final resistance. "I'm telling you in plain Greek."

"Say it without letting your teeth show."

"Are you going to leave me alone?" Manolis said, pretending to show anger and displeasure so as not to laugh.

"No, say it without laughing!" Saitonicolis repeated.

Then, Manolis could no longer restrain himself, but again he turned his laughter into indignation.

"What do I want a sweetheart for if they don't let me see her?"

"Let go of that chair, son!" Saitonicolis shouted, seeing that Manolis' stubborness was being vented on it. "It's not to blame."

Then he went on:

"The clever one wanted to be allowed to stay night and day at Thomas' house. And, because his will isn't being done, he has become sluggish and has begun wandering on the rooftops and in the streets like a madman, throwing stones and words and breaking pitchers. I, too, loved your mother before we got married and I hardly entered their house except to get engaged to her. I wouldn't raise my eyes to look at her in front of others. Isn't that the truth, Reginio?"

"True, d'you expect lies?"

"Only when dancing would I go so far as to sing her a *mattinada*[51] full of innuendo and she would answer me with statements full of allusions. Love requires prudence, humility ... Doesn't the song say it too. This is how honourable men behave Manolis."

Reginio sighed and she began to muse about a distant time from which the echo of the couplet came to her:

I revel in your eyes
When you turn them down.

Saitonicolis interrupted her musings; excited with his own

102

memories, he called to her to bring him "a drop of wine." In the end, Manolis, too, promised that he would stop his bizarre behavior, and Reginio went out to put out the mattresses on the roof where they had been sleeping since the weather began getting warm. Next day, Manolis went out with praiseworthy intentions. But a little later when he met Pighi returning from the river, his stubborness strangely revived and, averting his face, he went on without greeting her.

"Did I hurt you so much?" Pighi said, stopping.

"I don't want you to talk to me! Manolis answered harshly, without turning around, and left, quickening his pace as if he were being pursued. As he was going away, he was saying to himself: "I don't want you to talk to me . . . What the devil, should I love you by force? Take Tereres so that your brother's will is done. I don't want you, dear, how else can I say it? . . . There are other girls in the village who are a thousand times better. Are you better than Marouli?"

Walking, he left the village without realizing it.

Sudddenly he heard a familiar female voice, greeting him from a distance and turning around he saw Zervoudhena walking toward him. The window had a basket on her arm and was walking with her usual quick step. Hardly a day went by without his seeing her at least once; someone more attentive than Manolis would have come to the conclusion that the widow was trying to meet him. While other days, meeting her didn't bother Manolis, that day it worried him.

Paradoxically, though, Kalio didn't appear to be angry.

"Where to, Manolio?" she asked him.

"I'm going up to Mavriko to tie the mule in another place," said he.

"I'm also going to Mavriko to gather pumpkin blossoms for dolmades.[52] Just wait a bit so we can go together and I can tell you something."

Manolis waited for her.

"Do you know that we're going to quarrel, Manolio?" the widow said when she caught up with him.

And in a motherly tone, but rather unreprovingly, she told him never to bother her daughter again. She said she loved him as if he were her own child, but she also couldn't help being angry with him over his conduct toward her daughter. Since he was about to marry Pighi and had been betrothed what did he want with her daughter? . . He had already eaten his cake, so to speak. But let bygones be bygones, she forgave him since it was the first time; but if he bothered her daughter again, they would have a rough time of it. Marghi herself would not permit herself to be bothered again and she was capable of breaking his head with a stone.

"It doesn't matter," Manolis said smiling and blushing at the same time. "I'd like her to break it. Her stones would be as light as her hands."

"Come to your senses, Manolis," Kalio told him, trying to seem severe, though inwardly she was not displeased by Manolis' boldness. "These are ugly, unsuitable things and you must stop them. You're going to marry one woman, not two. And that fine-feathered father of yours chose the one you're going to get. You must leave your sweet talk for Pighi and not bother other girls because you're going to get in trouble . . . Ah! If you weren't bound to the Thomases, or if you had broken the agreement, then I'd give my consent for you to marry Marghi with all my heart. . . ."

"I've broken it, but my father won't."

And with complete guilelessness, he related everything that happened between him and the Thomases, and even everything that had been said with his parents the night before.

Kalio agreed with Manolis and encouraged him in his belief that he was a victim. She knew how headstrong and rude the Thomases were. His father sure knew how to throw him in with good kin. They used to say that Pighi was kind, but -- may God forgive me -- she couldn't help resembling her father and her brother a little. This head of lettuce comes from the same garden. Saitonicolis didn't act wisely by throwing his child into such a family of pigs. And anyway wasn't Manolis so much sought after that he could find both another girl and property? What did he like in the Thomases, their wealth or their good breeding. They say that a child shouldn't do anything against his parents' will. But if the parents don't see what's right and are going to burn their child, then the child should do whatever he thinks is right, it seems to me."

"I think that's what I'm going to do," Manolis said thoughtfully.

And after a few moments of silence, he asked hesitatingly:

"But, . . . do you want to give me Marouli?"

Kalio looked at him with a profound inquiring gaze.

"Break up with the Thomases . . . I've told you that I want it with all my heart."

"And Aunt Kalio, does Marouli want it too?" Manolis said in a voice trembling from emotion.

But if the unfortunate young man could have imagined the

mistake he made in the choice of a term to express his respect for the widow, his excitement would have been transformed into despair.

Kalio could not hide her displeasure. The word "aunt" struck her like a slap. She almost told him that he was a blockhead and a dunce and that he should get off her back. He wanted to get married though he could not distinguish a young woman from an old one. He called a thirty-year old woman, auntie, as if she were sixty. But her indignation gave away almost immediately before the charm which Manolis' blooming youth exerted over her heart. If the young man's tongue had made a mistake, his youth and his impressive physique which rose in front of her, full of life and strength, were enough to forgive his every mistake in the eyes of a woman who knows what a man is. For her, Manolis, with all the faults of his inexperience and carelessness, was the ideal man.

"What can I tell you since you infuriated her with your conduct," Kalio said in a voice in which her displeasure could still be discerned. Wait till you disentangle yourself from the Thomases."

There they had to separate and Kalio turned towards her garden. It was a cheerful summer morning, but the widow walked sadly among the joys of nature. Instead of being pleased, she appeared to be dissatisfied wih Manolis' eagerness to give in to her efforts. Even she herself could not explain the state of her soul. While she walked though the vegetable garden, picking yellow blossoms, she was followed by the rustling of the abundant, dewy leaves, she felt a heaviness in her chest which caused her to sigh. "Strange thing!" she said to herself. "What's wrong with me? What's this uneasiness that has come over me?" And, ceasing to gather blossoms, she stood still for some time looking down at the open stretch of meadows, without seeing anything, absent-mindedly, staring blankly. A vague perturbation constricted her heart. And at the same time, the first lines of an old song which she had heard in her childhood and which had remained, buried in the depths of her memory, came again and again to her mind incontrollably:

> A maiden gathered blossoms
> And tore the petals one by one.[53]

The lower part of the valley was still covered by the white veil of the morning mist, which the sun thinned out and dissolved little by little. Harvesting had begun and half-harvested fields and the golden mounds of the haystacks could be seen. The harvesters, male and female, had already begun their work at dawn. The herdsmen, too, had led their animals very early in the morning into the reed thickets and to the edges of meadows to graze. From the moment the cuckoo's voice was heard, and the heat became more intense, the animals started to get touchy. For this reason, the herdsmen hastened to finish with the grazing before the hottest hours began so that, they could shut the animals in the cowsheds, the large enclosures shaded by plane-trees.

Astronomos, harvesting in one of the fields, interrupted his work and observed the mist. He shouted to Barbarezos, who was in a neighboring field:

"There's going to be a plague again. Disease for people as well as plants."

"How do you know this?" Barbarezos asked, rolling a cigarette.

"Can't you see the haze?" Astronomos said stretching his arm toward the mist.

"Yes, I see it."

"It's all malignant and it would be best to fumigate the beans."

"Wouldn't it be good to fumigate ourselves, too, so that the sickness doesn't get us?" Barbarezos said, taking out his "artillery" to light the enormous cigarette he had constructed. "This is what I'm going to do with the smoke. Come on, man, why don't you drop this aimless chatter? Every summer this mist comes in the morning."

"But do you ever wake up in the morning so you can see what's happening?" Astronomos answered, offended. "Even today since the sun found you awake so early, some old woman may die.

Barbarezos turned his back contemptuously without giving an answer, and went on smoking sitting on the soft grass at the edge of the field. However, someone else, in an adjacent field, just to aggravate things, said Barbarezos was right, that mist was nothing but the evaporation of the dew which fell at night and that this happened regularly every summer.

"I'm from here too, they didn't bring me here from Paris. But this mist is not like the others. It carries a yellowness like slime does."

"I can't see any yellowness," the other said, "so I think you're dreaming, Nicolis."

They paid no more attention to the foolish Astronomos who left his work to sit and study the color of the morning mist or the movement of the clouds. Practical people placed him in the same category as the indolent Barbarezos who came down to work one day, as he said, and all the 'work' he did was to roll cigarettes and smoke.

But after a little while, a shout made everybody turn to see

Manolis, at a distance, pursuing a fleeing mule which kicked and stirred up clouds of dust. Since the time he carried stones for the house, the mule had become so scared of Manolis that when it saw him approaching in order to tie it elsewhere to graze, it broke the stake to which it was tied and ran away terrified. Manolis chased it, swearing and throwing big clods of earth at it, since there weren't any stones in the pasture. Finally Manolis managed to catch the stake, which the mule was dragging at the end of the rope and, with a strong pull, he managed to stop the animal.

"Isn't it strange?" Astronomos said. "If it were Tereres, who's a runt of a man, Manolis would be scared of him, but he doesn't fear the mule which could kill with one kick."

This wise man also gave the following explanation of the whole thing. Because he had lived most of his life with animals, he wasn't afraid of them. However, he was afraid of men because he didn't know them.

When Manolis caught the stake the sun was directly overhead and the heat of the day had begun. His curiosity was drawn at the upper end of the fields, to a bucolic scene, and he stopped there. Several young herdsmen had surrounded a bull at a distance and were goading it. They were dancing and shouting:

> Come out, fly leave the dirt lump
> And climb into the ox's rump
> Make him explode
> And take the mountain road
> Cou-cou! Cou-cou! Cou-cou!

The herdsman to whom the bull belonged tried to stop them, pleading, swearing, chasing one child and then another, and finally he began to cry while the others continued to recite the refrain of the fly. One girl in particular, barefoot like most of the boys, and dusky both by nature and from the sun, would not stop, but jumped wildly, repeating:

> Come out, fly, leave the dirt lump
> And climb into the ox's rump.
> Cou-cou! Cou-cou! Cou-cou!

"Katerinio!" the herdsman shouted and dashed towards her. Screaming she eluded him by running among the grazing animals and hiding now behind one and then another herdsman. However, if she happened to stop for a moment, the others would move on, and so her voice would be heard again shortly.

Pausing, Manolis followed the scene with interest and laughed, joining from a distance in the merriment of the herdsmen. To be sure, if he had not been hindered by a wide ditch, it was quite possible he would have gone closer and taken part in the bucolic dance.

In the meantime, the bull began to be uneasy, shaking his tail vigorously and flaring his nostrils. Then, aroused, he raised his tail like a banner and took off running with all his strength. The herdsman ran after him shouting, "Nia! Nia!" but quickly saw that he was wasting his effort. Stopping, he watched the exasperated bull getting farther away, leaping over ditches and entering the fields and reappearing with his tail constantly raised. A few of the reapers, whom he was approaching, attempted to stop or turn him back by shaking their scythes; most of them excited him more by shouting: "Cou-cou, "Cou-cou!"

But the herdsman, to whom the excited bull belonged, hearing Manolis' voice, turned to him wrathfully and shouted:

"You go to the devil, too, Patouchas."

Manolis became furious and charged the herdsman, but his impetus was slowed by the ditch. It was so wide that if he tried to leap across it he would fall in the water, which was of considerable depth. He looked around but could not find a stone and, not having a rock to throw at the insolent herdsman, he fired a threat at him.

"Okay, buster, I'll catch you some other time and I'll teach you who Patouchas is."

However, in a corner of the pasture, where the herdsmen were, there was a pile of rocks and when they saw that Manolis was unable or dared not leap across the ditch, they rushed to the rocks and began to stone him. And swarthy Katerina took a lively part in that rock fight. Manolis, after being hit in the chest by several pebbles, was obliged to retreat and repeat his threat from a distance, while the herdsmen shouted after him:

"Cou-cou . . . Cou-cou, Patouchas!"

The derisive "nickname" reminded Manolis of Tereres, and all of his annoyance turned against the magician, to whom he attributed the invention and diffusion of the scorn which he now encountered everywhere, in the village and even in the pastures. While thinking of how to avenge himself, he remembered his mother's words, that if he renounced Pighi he would be doing what Tereres wanted. Thus, precisely because he wanted to exasperate Tereres, he had to marry her. Well, he would exasperate that ugly character, Tereres. He would insist on getting Pighi, by God, even if it meant waiting ten years. It is certain that, since the preceding evening, his sentiments had once again been directed toward the daughter of Thomas. But in the morning when he saw her again, he was suddenly overcome with the obstinacy of a child, when it is given an object which it has been demanding persistently.

The widow found him in this psychological state a little later, and it was not difficult for her to bring him under her influence. But the change was not genuine. Pighi, so shy and reserved that the stubborn and frivolous Manolis could not feel her presence, retained her place in the depths of his heart. It is true that since he noticed the widow's daughter, Marghi's pale and delicate charms exterted another kind of attraction on the heart of the semi-wild adolescent. Whenever he saw her, a savage force pushed him to enclose her in his strong arms and melt that dainty, milky-white blonde in the excessive heat of his passion. But it is certain that without the Thomases' strictness, his attention would perhaps never have turned to Zervodhopoula, even with the persistent efforts of the widow.

His real preference was Pighi. She dominated his thoughts even when stubborness pushed him towards the other or others. On that day Marghi dallied a moment in his imagination, but as soon as he and Zervoudhena separated, Pighi appeared and displaced her. In the place of the cold and pretentious Marghi, Thomas' daughter appeared in his thoughts humble, sad and pleading. And she was telling him a quiet and frightened voice: "What have I done to you, Manolio, why don't you talk to me and why don't you turn around to look at me? Is it my fault if my brother is cruel and ill-natured? Doesn't that hurt me too? If you only knew what I am going through . . .! If Stratis is mean, can you say anything bad about me? If you only knew what I have to put up with. Are you going to let them marry me to Tereres and make me miserable? Don't you feel sorry for me?"

Imagining these things, Manolis was moved to tears and said:

"But for what is she to blame, the poor soul . . .? No, Tereres, I'm not going to let you take her; better, the devil take you."

Upon returning to the village, instead of going out of his way to avoid Thomas' house, he walked straight to it.

"And after all," he continued, talking to himself. "I'm not going to get married to Stratis, like my mother says. As soon as we get married and go to our house, let him dare come. Out, out of here, you poisonous tongue. Pighi was your sister till last night; today and, from now on, she is my wife."

However, the thought of the house tended to cast a shadow on his brave resolutions. If this house were completed, his troubles would be over. But it had no end to it. The first floor was almost done, but Saitonicolis insisted on building a second floor and so another winter would pass, and if the rain interrupted the work, spring would come and . . . here comes May. A few days before, he dared say to his father that the first floor was enough, but Saitonicolis did not want to hear anything of it. He knew what he was doing. If a job has to be done, why not do it right? He was marrying his son only once and so he wanted to build him a proper house, not a hut as if he were the child of some beggar. And with these excuses, whose importance Manolis could not understand, and which he could not dispute, the building dragged on, and for that reason his troubles would not end.

When he arrived before Thomas' house, the noise of the loom interrupted his melancholy thoughts. Stopping below the window, he coughed; Pighi, recognizing his step, had already jumped up from her loom and her face appeared among the flowers in the window. From the girl's speedy appearance, Manolis understood she was alone, but not taking any chances, he asked if her father or brother were there. He gave the excuse that he wanted to tell them that while he was at the meadow, several animals had damaged their crops and that they should go "estimate" the damage in order to ask for compensation.

"No, they're both out. If you still don't dislike me, come in."

Manolis entered blushing with shame and joy.

"Welcome to the angry one!" Pighi said, radiantly.

And, after offering him a chair, she sat opposite him on the bench of the loom.

"I thought you wouldn't talk to me again . . ." she continued. "In the morning when you passed by me and didn't turn around to look at me . . . Didn't you hear me speak to you?"

Manolis lowered his eyes and did not answer.

"You heard me but you wanted to make me unhappy. Only I know how much you hurt me."

"I just did it, I was just kidding," Manolis said laughing and blushing at the same time.

"Ah, just kidding . . . you did it out of spite . . ." said Pighi shaking the lamp, "Okay, smarty!"

"But what did you expect? Shouldn't I be angry after all that your brother told me?" blurted Manolis suddenly.

"No, I didn't say you weren't in the right. But my brother's mistake wasn't mine. What can I say since he's my brother?"

"What do you want me to do when he tells me to never come to your house again and never speak to you again?"

"Don't hold it against him, he's hot tempered, but he's not bad. And, after all, why do you care . . .? Isn't it enough for you that I love you?" said Pighi, in a barely audible voice.

Manolis's eyes flashed.

"I love you, he said, "but can't you see how they don't let us."

"And you'll be passing again by our street so I can see you?"

"Is it possible for me not to pass by?" said Manolis and his face reddened, like a mass of red-hot iron.

"And you won't act mean to me again, okay?"

"Okay," answered Manolis and the voice came out of his breast like the exhalation of a seething cauldron.

And, in effect, he was boiling and seething within and in the end he was off his chair. He stood up and, approaching the loom, he rested his arm on the corner. However, his approach increased Pighi's excitement; in her confusion she turned around and, putting her feet on the pedals, she took the shuttle in her hand. Her hands trembled. Manolis bent over her and she felt his warm breath on her neck.

"My soul, Pighio, how beautiful you are!" he whispered close to her neck.

The girl drew back a little on the bench and, turning around, looked at him with a sly smile:

"More beautiful than Zervodhopoula?" she said to him.

"No, no," Manolis said hiding his face with his hands.

"Didn't you tell her the same things, too?"

"I'm not going to do it again . . . my God and soul, I'm not going to do it again."

"And you don't love her at all, not even a bit?"

"Not a bit."

"Do you swear?"

"Didn't I say my God and soul?"

Pighi crossed her fingers and offering the cross to Manolis, she said to him:

"Kiss there!"

Manolis leaned over, but after kissing the cross he switched to her cheek. Pighi tried to push him back but Manolis was now unrestrainable.

"Pighio," he whispered, "it's you I love and nobody else."

His strong arms enclosed her while his lips sought her lips.

"Let go, Manolis . . " said Pighi, trying to escape. "Somebody might come . . . Let go of me, I tell you. If you love me . . ."

Finally, slipping out of the embrace, she fell inside the loom where the pedals were. Manolis' erotic excitement would have followed her there. That is, the loom ran the danger of breaking into pieces and the woof being cut. But all these disasters were averted by a familiar voice:

"Are you there, my child Pighio?"

"My mother . . .!" Manolis said, getting away from the loom.

"The shame!" Pighi whispered, exiting from the loom press, all dusty, with her dress and hair in disorder.

When Reginio came in, she was spinning.[54] Realizing that she had arrived at an unsuitable moment, Manolis' mother was also overtaken by confusion, indeed she blushed and did not not know what to say. Manolis standing next to the wooden column, which supported the roof, was looking at her as if he was seeing her for the first time; Pighi was so confused that she began going back and forth, looking for a chair for her future mother-in-law, while there were two in front of her.

"Wouldn't Stratis be justified in scolding you, Manolis, if he came now?" Saitonicolina said.

"So let him cone," Manolis answered with provocative stubbornness. "If he had come, what would he have done?"

Pighi alternately blushed and paled from embarassment, and Reginio, in order to give her time to recover and arrange her dress and hair, went near the window and stood admiring the flowers in the flower-pots; touching some basil and smelling its aroma, she said:

"I love the way this curly basil smells!"

Then turning towards the Plaka where, below the road, the tombs of the Turks were, she said:

"Dear, which dog died?"

"Ladhobraimis," Manolis informed her, also approaching the window. "When I passed by the mosque, they were chanting the funeral service."

After a while, Pighi, too came near and the three of them watched the Turkish funeral. The distance was not great and even the *davout* in which the dead man was enclosed, could be discerned. The imam, a very short man wearing a turban, went first. This was a doubly pleasant spectacle for Saitonicolina. First, because it meant one

Turk less, and second, because Ladhobraimis was a personal enemy of her husband. Because their lands abutted, they had frequent confrontations and quarrels. Once Saitonicolis was jailed for several months because he gave him a beating. "But Ladhobraimis was so badly injured that he needed help to get around," Reginio explained.

While she was enjoying the spectacle of her enemy's funeral, the two young people standing on either side of her exchanged secret glances. Manolis was biting his finger out of spite because Pighi had escaped from him because his mother's visit had come at such an inconvenient moment.

"Have a good trip, Agha Brahim!" Saitonicolina was saying, without taking her eyes from the Turkish monuments. "There, they're putting him in the grave. He's going . . . he's going to the devil and his bones have already turned to pitch. Can you see? Do you see, Manolis?"

"They've buried him," Manolis said. However, he would have preferred that Stratis, instead of Ladhobraimis, were the one buried. The thought of Stratis began to worry him so that whenever he heard steps in the street he became agitated.

"Take some more aghas, many more, with you, Agha Brahim," Saitonicolina said, "to keep you company! There, they've covered him up and they're leaving."

"And who's the one who's remained by himself? The imam?" Pighi asked.

"Yes he's praying over him and then he'll shout at him: "Mi sasirma oghloum.""[55]

Reginio explained that, according to Turkish belief, Isdraelis appears at the last moment to the person who has departed for the next world. The imam informs and encourages him so that he won't be disconcerted and make the mistake of taking the path of the unfaithful, which, naturally, would lead him to hell.

"And who's this Isdraelis?" Manolis asked, beginning to imagine him something like Thomas.

"The angel of the Turks who carries off souls. There, look, look at how the Imam is leaving, he's running so hard he's almost flying. And he doesn't look back from fear."

Manolis watched the tomb, waiting for the terrible Isdraelis to come down. Then he said:

"I can't see any Isdraelis or any devil. Can you see him, Pighio?"

"Only the imam can see him," Reginio explained.

While Manolis waited to see the Turkish collector of souls, he saw someone equally frightening. Thomas was coming down Mount Kavalara loaded with willow twigs with which baskets and hampers are woven. Manolis thought it prudent that he should make his departure as quickly as the Turkish imam's from the tomb.

But his hope that he could continue the interrupted game did not last long. When, on the next day, he passed by Thomas' house, he found the old man weaving baskets while sitting under the mulberry tree which shaded the windows. Next day Thomas was in the same place and continued his weaving. The days went by and became weeks, while the rounded fez of the fear-inspiring old man seemed to be nailed to the spot, like the scarecrows which keep birds and animals from vegetable gardens. Manolis rarely saw Pighi and then only from a distance at the window, and when she went to the fountain or to vespers. And, in any case, she was also helping Stratis now with harvesting and threshing and rarely remained in the village. Beside Stratis she was more inacessible than with her father. First despair and then wild indignation overcame Manolis in succession. Whenever he passed by with the hope that the old man's weaving would have ended, he would see the rounded fez still in its place. Shaking with anger, he would whisper: "Haven't you gotten lost yet, the devil take you!" If his love for Pighi, or, even more, his fear of Stratis, had not restrained his wrath, the old man would perhaps have caught a stone on his old head so that his endless weaving and day and night shift would be over.

One evening he managed to speak with Pighi in the street, as she was returning from the fountain.

"This is no life", he said to her. "Is your father going to be weaving much longer? What does he want with so many baskets and hampers?"

"He wants to take them to Mesara to sell them."

"At that rate, here comes May, and June ..."

After a moment's thought he said to her, "Let me ask you, Pighio, would you like to elope?"

"And where shall we go?"

"To the mountains where we have our animals. Wherever we go we'll be fine, since we'll be together."

"I can't act against the will of my father and brother. So why don't you be patient?"

Manolis was jolted when he heard the word patience, a concept he could not yet understand and which he considered impossible, in his case.

"I don't have any patience, that's all I can tell you. Are you coming?"

"I can't," Pighi answered and, hearing steps, she went away.

"Very well, but you'll regret it," Manolis said, turning in the opposite direction.

But he said it without conviction, because he felt it was he who would regret it instead. The idea of spurning Pighi now seemed impossible to him. Even if such an idea came to him again, one glance from Pighi would be enough to bring him back. Those black eyes by now exerted an all-powerful spell on his soul. It seemed to him that those eyes had something which other eyes did not. The face, the stature, the movements and the voice of Pighi he could find in other women too, but not her eyes. He decided to fall down at his father's feet and beg him to hasten his union with Pighi and to tell him straight out that life without her was impossible, that he would go crazy. But when he would see his father he would lose his courage. And, at night, while the others slept, he would cry and tell his grief to the stars, in whose twinkling he saw the sweet sparkle of Pighi's glances and smiles.

Meanwhile, Thomas' fez continued to be nailed in the same spot. Sometimes the old man, seeing Manolis passing by, would call to him, but he always talked about boring things, about agriculture and basket weaving, about stones and wood, but rarely would he ask him to sit down. But while Thomas was giving him lessons about fertilizers and grafting wild trees, Manolis observed a big stone at the end of a wall rising above the rounded fez and thought what a heaven sent event it would be if, suddenly, that stone were to fall.

That red fez, which became redder from day to day, dyed by the falling mulberries, irritated him the way bulls are irritated by the red cloth waved by bull-fighters. When Manolis saw it, all the blood went to his head and he would be overcome by an urge, which he could resist only with difficulty, to throw a stone at him. When the old man would call him to give him agricultural advice, he would depart so possessed by annoyance that he could not see. He would go swearing and venting his anger on the animals he met on the road.

One day, at such a moment of irritation, he met Tereres outside the village and, without any prologue, grabbed him by the neck so hard that poor Anagnostes' hand became paralyzed and let fall the ax he was holding.

"Are you the one who's boasting that he's going to bind me?" Manolis shouted as he lifted him in the air.

"In the name of God!" Tereres stammered in a half-choked voice.

But Manolis took the rope from the pack-saddle of Tereres' mule, at first, with the idea of tying him to the mule's tail and then whipping the animal so it would take off dragging the magician behind it. The idea of this revenge came to him from the memory of a fable which he had heard in his childhood. But the mule, as if it guessed his terrible plan, exploded, kicking twice in the air and left, running. Then Manolis changed his plan and, binding Anagnostes' hand and foot like a billy-goat, hung him from an overhanging branch of an olive-tree.

"I'll teach you how to bind!" he said to him.

And he continued his way to the meadows, running furiously and aimlessly, like a goaded bull.

Saitonicolis was pleased by Tereres' punishment although it did not seem to him to be sufficient, and he saw to it that it was completed the following day, by punching the magician when he heard him threatening once again that he would do this or that, among a crowd of villagers to whom he showed the black marks which the rope left on his hands and feet, and related how he was saved from hanging by Astronomos who happened by pass by in time.

After this feat of valour, Manolis thought it was the right time to talk to his father. And, at the first opportunity, he told him without preface or digression:

"Father, I want you to get me married . . . . I can't hold out any longer not even being able to see Pighi. If I don't marry her this month, my mind'll leave my head".

Saitonicolis watched him speechless for a few moments, after which he said to him severely:

"What's this you're saying? Has anybody else heard ever a son say to his father that he wants to get married because he can't hold out any longer?"

And then, angrily:

"Get out of my sight, you jackass, I don't want to look at you!" he said to him. "I had intended to get you married this coming Easter, but now neither next Easter nor the following one."

Manolis retreated timidly like a dog which fears being hit.

"All right," he whispered, "if I do something crazy again, you'll start shouting . . . ."

Yet the wretched lad persisted in his plea and instead of turning aside, he appealed to his mother with confidence that at least she would not talk to him harshly like his "master" and that, perhaps, she would succeed in lessening his unhappiness. Until then his mother had never seen him so bold nor so unhappy. He sat next to her and related his suffering and grief, how Thomas had installed himself in front of the door and it was impossible any more for him even to look at Pighi. Leaning against the folds of her dress, he cried like a child and implored her to mediate between him and his father and convince him to have the marriage performed as early as possible that month. His mother caressed him and tried to console him, but, at the same time, she showed him that it was impossible for the marriage to take place so soon because Pighi did not have her dowry ready.

"I don't want a dowry!" Manolis said animatedly. "What am I going to do with a dowry?"

"But it's not right my child . . . . Are we gypsies? The girl can't get married if she doesn't have everything she needs, otherwise the village will make fun of her."

She managed, though, to soothe Manolis' despair by promising she would mediate so that the marriage could take place as soon as possible, in two or three months at the most. But Saitonicolis was unyielding. Either the coming Easter or never; and, furthermore, the marriage itself would not take place during the Paschal season, but only the formal engagement which would be followed by the marriage two months later.

Then Manolis thought again of setting off for the mountains and breaking off all relations with people. But he was not slow in realizing that it was impossible for him to leave the village again. He was bound. Like golden chains, the rays from two black eyes held him there, bound and enslaved. Instead of making for the mountains, he went out and wandered through the streets of the village, thoughtful and gloomy. His steps automatically brought him before Thomas' house, where for the first time he did not see the fez which has brought him to despair. Instead, he saw Pighi standing at the door scattering barley to a swarm of chickens whose pecking on the dry ground made a noise like that of falling rain. Never before had Pighi appeared to him more attractive than at that moment, when the rosy reflection of the setting sun fell about her. The moment Manolis began moving towards her, he heard noise at the window and turning around, saw Thomas' fez bending forward between the basil and heard the old man's grumbling voice say:

"Are you going to be feeding the chickens all year? Come inside where I want you to be."

Manolis turned to marble. Pighi, casting the remainder of the barley in her apron to the chickens and her most melancholy glance at Manolis, disappeared. Thomas greeted Manolis with the smile of a wolf and probably would not have lost the occasion to give him one of his usual lessons had not Manolis hastened to get away. He left, cursing and vented his anger on an unfortunate dog which he kicked two meters.

A little later he met Zervoudhena.

"You look worried to me, Manolis," she said to him.

"Let me be," said Manolis, with a gesture of great anger.

"The Thomases must have done something to insult you again," said the widow. "You deserve it, getting mixed up with barbarians. But it's not your fault, you poor child. That fine-feathered father of yours is to blame."

"Yes, my father, my father, Kalio . . ." said Manolis, prepared either to cry or say disrespectful words against his father. In order to avoid doing one or the other, he started to leave, but the widow detained him and insisted on knowing the cause of his distress.

"Well," Manolis said finally, "they won't let me marry Pighi, or even look at her."

"Ay! And are we out of girls?" said the widow. "Are you going to sit around begging the Thomases, those hicks, you who are more than welcome wherever you ask? They don't want you once; you don't want them ten times over."

Manolis thought for a moment. Then he said:

"Yes, but I want Pighi."

The widow made a grimace of disgust:

"But why do you want her? Won't you tell me?"

"She's good. She's not like her brother, nor is she like her father."

"Do you know what an old proverb says? This lettuce comes from the same garden. She seems good now, but once you've tied the knot with her you'll see that she's the daughter of Thomas and the sister of that venomous Stratis. Good, he says? Well, can you tell me her good points? What of her beauty or her homemaking abilities? She doesn't have any of these. She was raised with oxen and she's an ox herself. If you want to yoke her to the plow, she'll be fine; but as a woman . . . After she's had a child, it'll disgust you even to take a golden apple from her hands. For your own good, because I love you, I tell you to take your hand back, now that they've given you a reason.

"But my father?"

"Don't listen to your father, because it's certain he's grown old and dotardly."

"But I can't, Kalio," said Manolis, in whose heart a struggle was clearly taking place. "I want Pighi . . . I love her."

"You love her . . .! But tell me, my child, what is it you like about that little cow? Her moustache? Can't you see that she has a moustache like a man?"

Manolis, until then, had not noticed the delicate down which flourished on Pighi's upper lip. At least it had not impressed him as a fault; rather in it he saw something charming and attractive. And, when on that down glittered diamonds of perspiration, he was possessed by a mad desire to sip that dew of her beauty with a kiss. But now that Zervoudhena presented the thing to him as a fault and as something unattractive, he began to think about it and to be disgusted. Was that, perhaps, a fault? But since it seemed beautiful to him . . .

"I like it," Manolis insisted.

"Ay, take her, my child, enjoy her," said Kalio with restrained spite. "Enjoy her moustache and her duskiness. What good is it for me to tell you, since you have eyes and don't see? I won't be sorry. I spoke to you for your own good; don't you hear? You'll be hitting your head. Take her, my child, and enjoy the mustachioed one."

The widow left him very depressed, soul sick. From then on her words worked on him like poison. In her effort to destroy his love, she afflicted and wounded the heart in which love had already put down roots. But, hard as Zervoudhena tried to blacken Pighi's image, Manolis never ceased to distinguish, beneath all the mud slung by the widow's words, the beauty and gentleness of the image. Only what she told him about the moustache left a persistent stain. Her words returned insistently to his mind; touching his own recently sprouted moustache, he thought that perhaps it was truly unbecoming for a woman to have this hair even so imperceptibly on her lip. That thought aroused indignation in his soul, and was directed at the widow instead. It seemed to him that he had been watching a beautiful dream and that she had awakened him in order to tell him something grievous and revolting.

That night he slept uneasily; his mother who was sleeping nearby heard him talking in his sleep:

"I told you I don't want you to say bad things about Pighi."

Manolis, despite all the difficulties his impatience encountered, did not despair entirely, but turned to his brother-in-law, to his aunts and uncles, begging them to convince his father to hasten the marriage. And he told everybody that he would go mad if the marriage did not take place soon. But everyone answered that it was shameful for him to say such things and that he had better be careful that the others did not hear him or he would become an object of scorn in the village.

Manolis was incapable of understanding the impropriety of his behavior and repeated:

"But why are they going to make fun of me? Is it shameful that I want to marry, since everybody marries?"

He had one last hope, either to convince Pighi that they go away, or for him to abduct her. But how would he speak to her? He saw her very rarely in the street, and then they managed to exchange only a few words. On one such occasion, before meeting her he had many convincing things to tell her, pointing out to her how pleasant life in the mountains would be, having the entire world beneath their feet and living alone, far from the annoyance and the evil of man, entirely free in their love to pass their days in the cool narrow valleys and to listen only to the chirping of the birds and the bleating of the goats, and climbing high peaks, from which could be seen the town and the sea, the wise plain of Messara, Kofina and Psiloritis, but when he would see her he forgot everything and only said to her:

"Come, let's go away, Pighio. Why won't you come?"

Thomas continued his endless work, which defeated Manolis' hopes, and never left his place except to transport the baskets and the hampers to the river in order to soak them. And, in order to dishearten Manolis completely, he announced to him one day his plan to set up a still in front of his house in order to manufacture *raki* from mulberries. Thus, to the manufacture of baskets was added another industry; this winter perhaps the repugnant old man would establish an olive press in order not to leave home.

Then the idea of abduction became steady and persistent in the spirit of the youth. He started to lie in wait at Pighi's door and to follow her everywhere in order to find an opportunity to talk to her and convince her. It was in vain that Karpathios became furious at his absences and Sykologos, between two psalms, said that it was not right that they themselves be both the builders and the helpers, and he threatened to leave the work half-finished and let Saitonicolis arrange things with his lazy son. But Manolis no longer gave heed either to the advice or the threats.

Even though his father reprimanded him after he learned of his absences from the builders, Manolis did not become more diligent. Saitonicolis, instead of insisting that Manolis keep working, sent a helper again, and restricted himself to saying that all shepherds are indolent like that, and if you take them away from sheep herding they are good for nothing.

One day, while Manolis was looking down from a high roof, he noticed Pighi heading downhill alone with a basket at her elbow. He followed her from a distance, and when he came out of the village, he suddenly found himself before her, with an imploring glance and a humble air, like a dog who fears it will be beaten.

"What are you doing down here?" the girl said to him smiling. "What happened to the building?"

"I can't work since I can't see you," said Manolis. "My mind isn't in my head."

"Where is it, then?" she said, with provocative coquettry.

"At your side," Manolis answered, with a sigh.

"Ay, for this reason you should do everything you can so the house will be finished soon . . . so I can finish my dowry soon."

"But I can't, I tell you, I can't, God and soul. Don't you believe me?"

And, rather from agony than from the heat, perspiration fell in large beads from both his forehead and his temples onto his bullish neck.

"I try to work and I fall into thought and I forget the work, and I'm always thinking of you and I want to see you, to hear your voice or at least the sound of the pedal of your loom. And then I leave everything and go off and wander in the alleys and streets as though I'm crazy . . . I can't anymore, Pighi, I can't . . . How long am I to wait? My father says the wedding will take place two months after Easter. Can I wait till then while your father is always at the door and I am unable to see you? I'll go to pieces, I'll go crazy." ·

"And what are we to do?" said Pighi, filled with distress too. "Since we can't do otherwise, we have to wait."

"I don't hold with waiting, just come so we can go away. As I told you, we can go to the mountains. If you like, we'll stay forever."

"Are you in your right mind to say we should go live forever up there in the mountains? What are we, wild animals?"

"Yes, I'm in my right mind when I say it. Do you think it isn't a thousand times better in the mountains than in the village? Wild animals, you tell me? Have you ever seen a wild animal?"

"No, I never saw one."

"Ay, the wild animals are a lot better than many people like Tereres, like . . ."

He almost added "and like your father and your brother."

"Wild animals," he continued bitterly, "don't behave cruelly towards people, and they don't bother those who don't bother them."

At that moment Pighi's upper lip was the way he loved to see it. And remembering the words of the widow, he came to the point of saying that, in the solitude of the mountains there would not be evil-tongued people who say she was "moustachioed," the way they called him Patouchas. But thinking that he would make her unhappy just as he was unhappy when he heard the nickname which they had attached to him, he suppressed his thought.

"And which priest is going to bless us?" Pighi asked.

"Which priest is going to bless us?" Manolis repeated, scratching his forehead.

But his confusion did not last very long.

"Nobody," he said. "If we elope, what do we care?"

Pighi's face, however, expressed horror.

"What are you saying, Manolio? Are we Turks to get married without a priest?"

"If they just permit us to get married, let them send even ten priests to bless us, I don't care. But since they don't let us . . .? There is no other salvation except for you to come so we can elope. If you want a priest, I could send a lamb and two or three pieces of cheese to Father Yorghos and he'd come a-fly-ing to bless us at the little church of Omalos."

"And the best man?"

"A shepherd. There are so many shepherds at Omalos. Then, if you want, we can come down to the village and the house will be ready. But if you ask me, I prefer to stay in the mountains forever and in winter we can come down with our animals to the beach and winter there. Don't you like that kind of life?"

"Whatever you like, I like."

"Then come, let's leave."

Pighi was thinking. Then she said:

"This can't be done, Manolio. Just have patience, like me. It's not right for us to go against our parents' will, because they will curse us, then things will never go well for us and we'll never get ahead."

Pighi's new objection threw Manolis' rhetoric into a momentary confusion. But then he said:

"They won't curse us because they love us. My father gets mad at me sometimes and shouts, but he's not cruel. I don't know about yours . . . ."

An echoing shot, from a short distance away, interrupted him. Two frightened turtle doves flew by as feathers fell from the wings of one.

"It must be my brother," Pighi said disturbed. "When he left the house he took his rifle and he must be hunting somewhere around here. We'd better not walk together, because if he sees us he'll kill us.

Manolis who was no less disturbed by the event, looked over a nearby wall and saw a Turkish hunter among the olive trees loading his rifle.

"It's Kaoukakis," he said, regaining courage.

And he went on walking with Pighi towards Livadia and he wouldn't stop begging her to go away with him.

"Do you want me to go crazy?" he said to her. "Is that what you want? You don't love me. If you loved me, you wouldn't torture me this way."

"Don't I love you?" Pighi was saying, ready to cry. "But what else can I do?"

Manolis became stubborn and began seriously considering carrying her off by force. Pighi's robust shape did not encourage such an undertaking. Her arms were capable of putting up tremendous opposition. But there was no other way out. Despair and stubbornness could double Manolis' strength. And while he kept on begging, reinforcing the persuasiveness of his tongue with the melancholy passion of his eyes, he recalculated the possibilities for the success of a violent attempt.

The road was deserted. Below there were olive-groves which were partially enclosed from the side of the road by dirt walls and rows of wild almond-trees, myrtle shrubs and bushes. A second shot echoed through the olive-groves and, after a little, there was another so near that they heard the noise of the shot in the foliage of an olive-tree. And Pighi, very upset, said:

"Go away, Manolis, in God's name. Go away if you love me, in case Stratis comes . . . ."

"It's not Stratis and don't be afraid," Manolis said, having looked over the fence again. "Haven't I been telling you? Come, let's go away and then we'll be free of Stratis, too. Listen." So he sang to her to make a point:

> Curse whoever finds time and waits for more.
> Because time changes things to the core.

"D'you hear," Manolis said, "how the song says it too . . .? Come, because for God's sake . . . even I don't know what I can do."

"I'm not coming Manolis, just go away, in case Stratis comes or anybody else sees us together," Pighi said in agony.

Manolis blushed with stubbornness.

"I'm not leaving. If we don't go together, just forget about it," he said. "We'll leave together, do you hear?"

He followed her to the garden where she was going. When Pighi drew the branch away which blocked the entrance to the vegetable garden, her hand was trembling. The decisiveness flashing in Manolis' eyes frightened her and the danger of Stratis' appearance worried her so much that she felt a compulsion to turn to flight. She was no less afraid of being seen with Manolis in the enclosed garden by some stranger.

"May you enjoy whatever you love and admire, Manolis," she said to him, crossing her hand over her chest, "may your parents and brothers live long, leave me and go away . . .! Go away . . .!"

She was so beautiful as she stood there entreating him; her black eyes, welling up with tears, were so charming that Manolis, instead of giving in, became more daring. He was so carried away that he forgot and despised every danger.

"My Pighio, my Pighio, my Pighio!" he exclaimed and the three "mys" sounded like three burning kisses.

At the same time, he rushed forward and embraced her, his mouth seeking her lips, uttering things flowing out of wild erotic paroxysm. The girl pushed him back and tried to avoid him by ducking her head. But what kind of strength could loosen the arms which were tight around her? That strength was found in the name which Pighi, seeing that her resistance was in vain, shouted:

"Stratis! Stratis!"

Manolis' embrace immediately loosened and Pighi, managing to escape, turned to flight. Manolis, having looked around and not seen Stratis, ran after her, and caught her at the edge of the field.

"Let me go, Manolis, otherwise I'll kill myself," the girl said, gasping, with eyes full of tears.

But Manolis could no longer hear nor see. She didn't want to go willingly? Then he'd take her by force. He grabbed her by the waist and lifted her like a child. And he was about to put her on his shoulder like a wooden beam and then head for the mountains, but his titanic decision was stopped by an unpleasant surprise.

"You dishonorable lout, Patouchas . . .!" a familiar voice roared from the fence.

It was Stratis, in the flesh this time, and frightening with the rifle he was holidng as he headed towards Manolis. Pighi, released by Manolis' paralyzed arms, stood facing him. For a moment Stratis hesitated whether or not he should kill them both. Then he shouted to his sister:

"Get out of here, so I don't kill you."

Pighi however, did not move and Manolis, losing all manly dignity in the face of the sudden danger, retired behind the girl lowering his head like a lark when it sees a stone coming toward it.

Then Stratis jumped over the fence and entered the garden. Pighi ran towards him shouting:

"Brother, brother, kill me!"

Putting her arms around him, she prevented him from using his rifle. Turning to Manolis at the same time, she shouted at him:

"Go away, go away!"

Manolis, who had been standing petrified and stupidly watching the fuming Stratis, took off, gradually increasing his speed. Once out of the garden and having found a bulwark behind the thick trunk of an olive-tree, he shouted at Stratis, who was still struggling with his sister.

"Goodbye for now, but just wait until I find you without a rifle!"

Pighi exerted superhuman force to restrain her brother and give Manolis time to get away. Stratis was pushing and hitting her, furious with anger, but she clung to him in a desperate effort to prevent him from pursuing Manolis. But when Stratis heard Manolis' challenge he gave her a violent push and she fell away in a heap. Then running to the edge of the garden and aiming his rifle at Manolis, who at that moment had left his fortification, Stratis pulled the trigger. Instead of a gunshot, the comic pop of failure was heard - no bullet! Manolis answered by stretching out his open palm at Stratis. But, just in case, he quickened his pace, and a minute later a thundering report made him jump. He felt a twinge of pain in his back-side which burned a bit like turpentine. It put wings on his feet, while his hand rubbed the wounded spot. Only when he had reached a distance from which he could ignore even a bullet, did he turn and see Stratis punching and kicking his sister inside the garden. The scene made him unhappy, but the memory of Pighi's stubborn refusals to his proposals gave his cowardice an excuse, and shrugging his shoulders, he said:

"She has it coming . . . let them go at each other."

Then his instinctive fear was followed by depression and much lamenting for the total disintegration of his hopes and dreams. All the surrounding world seemed to him like a dismal ruin in which he alone remained to grieve. And he felt like falling on the grass to cry and cry. Why did all these successive injustices happen to him? Why did people persecute him thus, since he neither hated nor bothered anyone? How had he wronged Thomas? In particular how had he wronged Stratis that he harassed him with such fury? What wrong had he done to those who attached a scornful "nickname" to him? He had been wounded twice that day, once by buckshot, the other time by the nickname which Stratis flung in his face in front of Pighi. Now he felt that the former was insignificant; a few pellets had just pierced his skin; the latter, however, had wounded him deeply. The frustration afflicting him was largely due to the beastly cowardice which he had shown and by which he had now been reduced to nothing. Perhaps, without that frustration, he could have had the quickness and the courage to confront Stratis' rifle as surely it wasn't impossible for him to attack and disarm him.

His depression and despair were so great that he almost doubted whether he was alive or just a shadow. He was walking like a ghost, and his strength had been drained to such a degree that one blow could have knocked him over. He imagined himself to be alone in the world, surrounded by general hostility and malevolence. Everybody worked together to harm him, including his parents and Pighi. Since he had come down to the village, he had not passed a day without being given more reason for bitterness. Whatever he did, whatever he said was wrong, and the others were always right.

His thoughts, little by little, led him to the conclusion that if Pighi had concurred sooner in his plan to abduct her, these things wouldn't have happened. Consequently she was the main reason for his unhappiness. Having reached this conclusion, his thoughts went on to a suspicion, which made Pighi even more guilty. Had she, perhaps, confessed his proposals to her brother and that disgusting person, being well informed, had followed them and appeared at the garden at exactly the moment he decided to carry out his decision? It was not long before that thought was transformed, by his simple and excited brain, into a conviction, and all his indignation and desire for revenge were directed toward both brother and sister. He, who, a few moments ago had strength only to walk, was now furious and grinding his teeth and shaking his clenched fists at Stratis and his sister. Zervoudhena was right in saying that they could not help but be alike. Oh, that moustachioed one!

He forgot the self-denial with which the one he now described as moustachioed, had put herself in the face of danger to save him, and the severity with which her brother dealt with her because of him.

He wandered in Livadia for quite some time, without seeing or hearing any of the goings-on around him; he walked, now slowly, and now quickly, depending on the vehemence of his feelings and thoughts. He automatically arrived at the threshing floor where at that hour Saitonicolis was winnowing. His mother was there, too, spinning yarn under the willow tree where harvesters usually rested in its shade. Manolis' unexpected arrival, and especially the agitation of his face, worried his parents. Reginio stopped her work, and Saitonicolis, too, left his wooden pitchfork and came near.

"What is it, Manolis? What are you doing down here?"

"I came to tell you that I am no longer going to get married or anything," Manolis answered in a greatly agitated tone.

"Here we are . . .! And how did this sudden decision come to you? Could it be that you quarreled with Stratis again?"

"I didn't quarrel with anyone . . . but I don't want to hear his name again or his sister's, or anyone else's in that pig-family! I don't want to know them any more."

The two parents exchanged a glance of surprise.

"But how did this come to you?" Saitonicolis asked.

"That's what I want," Manolis answered with spite.

"But you must have a reason. Won't you tell us?"

"There's nothing wrong with me, I just don't want to know the Thomases any more. That's all."

"The Thomases and Pighi too?"

"I don't want Pighi or any other girl."

"No other girl! And are you going to become a monk?" Saitonicolis said, trying to smile. "I don't believe it, my child. 'I'd go become a monk to save my soul, but the devil I have in my pants won't let me.' Do you know the song?"

"I don't know anything!" Manolis said, turning his face away and increasing his stubbornness in order not to laugh. "I'm not going to marry Pighi even if the sky changes places with earth. Just go and tell Thomas before I go and break all his baskets and hampers on his big fez."

"But you can't have changed your mind just like that. You must have a reason. How many days have you been chewing our ears to get you married because you were going out of your mind and talking to the mountains. . .?

"Ay, but now I don't want to."

"But why don't you?"

"Because I don't want to," the young man answered stamping his foot on the ground, "I don't feel like it. Do you want another reason?"

And after a moment he said:

"I don't want her because she has a moustache. What, are we both going to have moustaches so you can't tell the man from the woman?"

Then he left, not wanting to hear anything else.

"Does the Bourbas know what a date is?" Saitonicolis said, shaking his head, while he watched his son go away.

Then turning to his worried wife, he said to her:

"Don't worry, he'll get over it."

7

"It looks like a drunkard, but it isn't a drunkard. It walks like an ox but it isn't an ox. What is it?" Astronomos was saying a few months later at a merry evening gathering where they were posing riddles. And nobody could solve the unheard of riddle but Astronomos insisted.

"Come on, guess."

Finally Spyridolenia called out:

"I've got it . . .Patouchas!"

"Bravo, Lenio!" Astronomos said to her.

Everybody laughed at the successful caricature and said it was to be expected that Spyridolenia would recognize her godson as Astronomos presented him. And leaving the riddles, they began to talk about Manolis, who for some time had been a major topic of discussion. This was because Patouchas, as everybody now called him, appeared constantly to be drunk though he very rarely drank. He did not need wine to get drunk. He was inebriated by the juice, the rich juice of life, which circulated and boiled in his veins, the "craziness" as his father called it, and for which, alas, there was no suitable medicine. This craziness seemed to subside, lying dormant during working days since it was not given an opportunity to express itself, being subdued by the exhausting tasks which Saitonicolis again began to assign to him. But on Sundays and other holidays it reappeared with a force of a high-spirited horse set free after a prolonged period of confinement.

In the morning, shortly after the liturgy, a loud inarticulate voice, rather like that of billy-goat than that of man, was heard:

"Eh! Eh! Eh!"

And Manolis appeared, or rather rushed around from the rooftops to the crossroads where the villagers were gathered, wearing his Sunday best, all brand new, all azure blue felt, the side-split boots - the so-called *sardinia*. He also had a long Cretan dagger at his waist. If he happened to see Zervodopoula, even from a great distance, he was seized by a veritable mania. Emitting a sigh rather like a howl, he jumped from roof to roof or ran in the streets, like a typhoon, sweeping away with his hands and feet every stone that happened in his way, and kicking or punching the animals he met. As he passed by, the road would be in an uproar, animals turned to flight, hens flapped their wings with fright, children cried out in fear and ran away.

When he came near Marghi, he would draw his dagger and thrust it into walls and trees and cry out with a savage passion:

"How long . . .! How long must I wait?"

He did not say anything when he saw her with other women, but the sigh which accompanied his cries could have set a windmill in motion and the glances which he directed at the widow's daughter sufficed to express the tempest of his soul.

Everyone knew by now that Patouchas had broken all relations with the Thomases and that he was passionately in love with Marghi whose mother seemed to be quite willing to make him a son-in-law. But Saitonicolis, whenever he heard talk about his son's new attachment, would calmly respond:

I'm telling you that it's Pighi he loves and it's Pighi he's going to marry. You just see him acting moonstruck. He'll get over it soon."

When, after the incident in the garden, Manolis met Zervoudhena, he said to her:

"Hey! we've broken off with the Thomases and we've broken off for ever."

"Glory be to God," the widow said, unable to conceal her joy.

Manolis related to her in detail what happened between him and Pighi, the subsequent intervention by Stratis and the events which followed. But this time he modified the truth, saying that Stratis had not wounded him, but that he had escaped by a hair. Feeling ashamed of his cowardice, he made up a feat of valour just to tell to the widow, that after Stratis had shot at him, he drew his dagger and charged him, that he would have slaughtered him like a billy-goat if Pighi had not intervened, and that with her help her brother found time to save himself by fleeing. Manolis did not neglect to mention his suspicion that Pighi was in collusion with her brother. In any case, in her persistent refusal to accept his kidnapping proposals, she was the reason for the danger in which he found himself.

"Do you see how my words one by one come true, like those from the pen of the scribe?" the widow said triumphantly.

By affirming that Manolis was right -- and when was he not right? -- she reinforced his suspicions and his unjustified and unreasonable indignation against Pighi.

"So, do you want to give me Marouli," Manolis said, "and make the Thomases burst from spite?"

"Since you broke all your bonds with those hicks, the thing is going to be easy. Marghi says she doesn't want you; but all girls say no in the beginning, then slowly, slowly they say yes. With time the sour grape turns sweet."

Once again Manolis ceased passing through Thomas' street and diligently avoided every possible meeting with Pighi. On the other hand, he sought every possible opportunity to see the widow's daughter. But their first meeting proved that the "sour grape" was excessively sour. Marghi was returning from church where she had gone to confession, when behind the church in a deserted spot at the end of the village, she found herself facing Patouchas. There was a blush on her normally pale and cold face, perhaps because she had confessed to the priest the secret feelings which Smyrnios aroused in her heart. That blush made her prettier than the crinoline or the gold trimmed pelisse. That day, she was dressed simply, but even on week days her clothing revealed care and attention which distinguished her from the others. When she saw Manolis, she raised her nose to the sky and decided to pass by without dignifying him with a glance; but Manolis had blocked the way and with a flirtatious complaint said to her:

"Won't you even say good day to me, Marouli?"

"Get out of my sight!" Marghi said, turning pale and stepping back.

"Say 'good day' to me and I'll let you pass."

"Go away, I tell you, don't make me sin right after I've come from confession," the girl insisted with even greater agitation.

Patouchas bent towards her in such a way that his hot breath fell on the girl's face.

"Did you tell the priest that I love you?" he whispered.

Marghi turned around to leave, but Manolis' arm reached in front of her like insurmountable wall.

"Don't you love me a little, just a little? Eh, Marouli, don't you love me just a bit?"

Then Marghi became furious and forgot all about confession, communion and Hell. Retreating to a nearby dirt wall, she picked up a large stone and raised it menacingly.

"Weren't you told, you ugly beast, not to talk to me again? Get out of my way before I turn your head into a distaff!"

Manolis, instead of going away, bent his head and said calmly.

"Go to it, Marouli. Even if your little white hands kill me, it wouldn't hurt me."

Marghi carried out her threat. But her white little hand was not strong enough and it trembled from anger and agitation, so the stone just grazed Manolis shoulder. He accepted the blow as if it were a caress and exclaimed with delight, "ooh-ooh-ooh!"

Marghi continued throwing stones furiously, but most of her projectiles missed their mark or did not reach the enemy, who after each blow repeated his exclamation of pleasure:

"Ooh-ooh-ooh! Your hands, Marouli. You have refreshed my heart."

Marghi, seeing that the blows of her anger smashed ineffectually on that rock, was ready to cry from spite.

"Let me pass, I tell you, you repulsive creature," she cried out, throwing a last stone at him.

Then rushing with all the force of her anger, she broke through the blockade.

Manolis didn't try to go afer her, but as he watched her go away, he said to her:

"Slowly, slowly the sour grape will turn to honey, so that the Thomases burst with jealousy."

In answer, Marghi extended her little white palm towards him with her fingers outstreched and said:

"Here's for your eyes!"[56]

Despite all the cries of pleasure with which he endured the stoning, Manolis was not especially pleased with the episode. No matter how feebly the stones were thrown by Marghi's soft hand, they had left painful traces on his shoulders and chest; he was hurt much more by the unrelenting hatred, expressed by the looks and words which she fired off with the stones. He was consoled, however, and emboldened by the memory of the widow's words. The sour grape would sweeten one day. Indeed, he was capable of waiting because Marghi was not guarded, like Pighi, by dragons with rounded fezes and rifles. He felt the absolute necessity of giving vent to his overflowing heart, even if only with words. He had, moreover, a special idea about the persuasiveness of his words, because he thought that his rude expressions of love communicated all the fervor which boiled within him. Indeed, he believed that Marghi's aversion to him would be incapable of resisting his passionate looks and words.

Perhaps he would have lost hope had he learned what occurred at the home of the widow shortly thereafter. Upon returning, Marghi gave free vent to her indignation, rage and tears. She was indignant because that coarse type insisted on calling her Marouli. She was furious because a rude Patouchas dared lift his glance as far as the level of her nose, and she wept at the thought that she had sinned only moments after confession and because her revenge had been totally ineffective against his thick hide. That thought changed her indignation to despair. And what would Yianakos Smyrnios say if he learned what happened? It would not have been at all unreasonable for him to assume that she had wanted and provoked what happened. What is certain is that Smyrnios continued to clean his hookahs and to occupy himself with his many tasks with a completely serene and calm conscience and heart, without suspecting at all that a tender heart was burning on his account and that in someone's little head, dreams, all of which concerned him, were being woven. Marghi, however, imagined that he not only knew, but also that he shared her love and that he was waiting from day to day to send her a matchmaker. Who else, beside her, could he possibly choose? But if he learned of the scene which took place behind the church and the previous one when Manolis broke her pitcher, was there not a danger that his love would be chilled and he would regret his choice?

The widow was neither aware of nor guessed the love which Marghi concealed in the depths of her little heart. For this reason she was unable to understand the insistent refusal which her daughter raised whenever she counseled her to not display such hostility toward Manolis, and extolled him as the best possible husband. But even if she had known that her daughter preferred Smyrnios, her astonishment would not have diminished, because to her mind, there was no possible comparison between Manolis and Smyrnios. What, did that thirty-year old, short, almost scrubby Smyrnios have to compare with Manolis?

Kalio too availed herself on that day of the opportunity to plead on behalf of Manolis. "My dear, come to your senses, and think that whoever takes Manolis will weave her life with a golden shuttle. You'll not find better, no matter what you say. In a man, kind-heartedness is the best thing. He'll never deny you a favor. And you'll have a man you can enjoy, who'll fill your house when he enters and the earth will tremble at his step. A man you'll enjoy, because he's not some unleavened, pallid pastry who'll die and leave you a widow at the crossroads."

Then Marghi thundered and flashed and swore on the bones of her father that she would drink poison if her mother so much as mentioned Manolis' name. And she cried inconsolably. Why did her mother wish, at all costs, to cause her misfortune? What sort of mother was she who wished ill for her daughter and pursued it with such persistence? In the name of God, was this a match for her, a villager like this, an ox? Was it for this that her mother had raised her with so much care and kept her from the sight of the sun? Is that why she sent her to the city, so she could marry her off to a wildman?

But Kalio's purpose remained unshakeable, and so she said, as had Saitonicolis:

"Does the Bourbas know what a date is?"

Later, sunk in thought, she sighed. Was she displeased because of her daughter's lack of judgement or from something else? Once, following such a sigh, some phrase rose to her lips, but it was immediately withdrawn to the depths of her heart and was registered only in her mind: "Ay, if only . . .!"

Meantime, Manolis continued quite zealously with his efforts to ripen the sour grape. Wherever Marghi went, especially during holidays, she met him standing before her; wherever she turned she met his flashing, but also pleading eyes.

Manolis loved her as much as he hated Stratis, Thomas and Pighi. His violent hate for them was transformed into violent love for the daughter of the widow. He loved her because he hated Pighi. The discontent, the impetuousness of his youth, which had almost been elevated to true love by Pighi's radiant eyes, forged in his thoughts all sorts of complaints against her. In any case, was it not reason enough to hate Pighi simply because she was the sister of Stratis and the daughter of Thomas? He loved, therefore, or wished to love, the widow's daughter, in order to spite the Thomases, as he said; but he also liked the girl because she was petite, pale, delicate, blonde and blue-eyed, in other words totally unlike him, a sunburned, dark-eyed giant. He was attracted to her by their differences just as he was attracted to Pighi by their similarities. For him, Marghi, had, aside from the attractions of a woman, the charm of a miniature work of art. In his hands she would be a plaything. Whenever he saw her, this impression gave him the desire to lift her in his arms, to enclose all of her in his embrace and to kiss her, to kiss her endlessly, to melt her in the flames of his passion. When he imagined the consummation of such bliss, the delicate blonde shivering in his arms, quivering beneath his burning kisses, he was overcome by paroxysms of passion. He was seized with impulses to run, shout, whinny, to knock over everything. He was no longer restrained by any modesty from announcing that he was crazy about the widow's daughter.

Marghi, however, not only did not love him, but could not even bear to see him and did not miss a chance to show it. One afternoon, as she was watering her plants, Manolis came by and asked for some basil, but instead of giving him basil, she threw the clay jug with which she was watering at his head. Manolis managed to avoid the clay jug, but did not manage to avoid its contents which soaked him.

"One for you and one for me, Marouli," he said laughing innocently.

He had soaked her when he had broken the pitcher, and now she had paid him back, so they were even.

Marghi's fine lips might have separated in a smile, if the incorrigible Manolis had not fallen once again into the teribble error of calling her Marouli. In vain the widow advised him to call her daughter by the name she had brought back from the city along with the crinoline. Aside from the fact that name was difficult for him to pronounce, he never remembered it in time.

Manolis withdrew, shaking his drenched clothing. When he found himself out of range, he directed toward Zervodhopoula a couplet in which he compared his being drenched to his love:

You grabbed the pitcher after setting me afire,
But now you can't quench the flaming pyre.

In another incident, however, Manolis' words managed to make her laugh. Marghi had come out on the porch and with a switch was driving away a donkey which had been eating the vine shading the front windows of their home. Manolis, appearing at that moment, became jealous of the donkey's luck at being beaten by those hands and shouted:

"Ah, to be a donkey!"

Marghi laughed.

"Aren't you one already?" she asked him.

"Your smile gives me joy! shouted Manolis.

Elated, because he was seeing the pretty little face smiling for the first time, he dashed forward and with a great leap climbed up to the high porch on which Marghi was standing. She barely managed to go in and shut the door in his face.

Saitonicolis learning of his son's feats, showed disinterest and would constantly say,

"It has to pass."

To his wife he would say privately that this was the way time would pass until Easter and then with a single word Manolis would become a lamb. Besides what could they do to him? Should they tie him up. He was neither an ox nor a horse.

"He can't be restrained. Even if you put him in chains he'll break them. Let's leave him alone so he can use up his craziness. Let him fight and get his lickings. He has to become more confident because he is still a bit of a coward, and it's a shame for such a youth to be scared. He doesn't do anything really bad, poor fellow. Stratis must have done something to him again and upset him. But when the time comes, I'll tell him one word, just one word, and he'll become a lamb."

Manolis' parents still did not know of the incident between him and Stratis in the garden, because both Manolis and Pighi had kept it quiet, the former being ashamed, the latter not wanting to condemn her brother and fearing that the whole thing could get out of hand and lead to an irreparable break. The gloomy Stratis was so laconic, that there was no danger of his saying anything, which would, in any case, jeopardize his sister's honor. The widow knew only a single distorted version of the events, from which the most important point, the pellets Manolis received on the most fleshy part of his body, was missing. Moreover, it was not in Kalio's interest to have it known that Manolis turned to her daughter only after the Thomases had shown him, especially in such a manner, that they did not want him.

Saitonicolis thought that breaking off was, in the end, a way for these incidents with Stratis and Thomas to stop, and thus the time until the wedding would pass peacefully and quietly. When it was time, it would not be difficult to get Manolis back in line, into some sort of discipline. In any event, there was nothing more they could say to advise him. When the father heard him repeat anew that he did not want Pighi, he was neither worried nor angry despite the exceptional stubbornness and decisiveness of his son's character and words. He did not even try to learn the cause of his recent revolt. What point would there be? He would hear the same things all over again, and who knows, even God would become angry with how far his anger would go, and after a few days, the same thing would happen as a result of Thomas' strictness or Stratis' peevishness, since it was impossible for him to ask people to allow his son the freedom he wanted. So he restricted himself to telling him:

"You don't want her, but I do, and when the hour comes what I want will be done. Until then do whatever you like, only don't forget that there is someone older than you. Now go."

The only thing that worried Saitonicolis was Pighi's suffering.

When he saw the girl who once was always smiling, lively and open-hearted, now all pale, weakened and melancholy, it broke his heart. Pighi tried to hide her pain and appear cheerful as she was in the past. But now her smile was bitter and in its bitterness Saitonicolis discerned the agony of jealousy which had begun to consume that innocent heart. He thought, however, that his assurance that Manolis could not marry anyone but the one he wanted would be enough to console her. She knew who Uncle Nicolis wanted, and she should also know that Manolis loved her, and that his aberrations were only acts of spite against the obstacles his love faced. When the obstacles were gone, the stubbornness would stop at once, and they would stop forever. In any case, Saitonicolis was the one holding the reins and he would not let his son take over. When he saw him overdoing it, he would pull in the reins. The freedom he allowed him was necessary so that his occasions for fights with Stratis would stop since as they gradually worsened, they could lead to something irreparable.

At each of their meetings Pighi tried to talk to him about Marghi, but an invincible bashfulness prevented her. Finally, one day, she managed to utter Zervodhopoula's name. . . .

"Uncle Nicoli, the whole world says he loves Zervoudhopoula."

Saitonicolis laughed:

"That tramp! Even if they were the last people in the world, he wouldn't marry that girl. Listen, Pighi, my child, to what I'm telling you. Gadfly's daughter cannot become Saitonicolis' daughter-in-law. Remember my words and don't worry about it."

However, months went by and the craziness did not subside; instead it increased. Saitonicolis pretended to not know about Manolis' aberrations, and Manolis avoided talking with his father as much as possible. Often, after dinner, he would go out to meet his friends on the rooftops or to evening gatherings, where the *Erotokritos*[57] was being read, and where riddles and tongue twisters were posed. At other times, when he feared unpleasant exchanges with his father, he ate and slept at his sister's home.

When the time set for the wedding neared, Saitonicolis thought it was time to pull in the reins, as he put it. But this was not as easy as he had imagined. One day, in order to sound out his intentions, he announced to Manolis that the number of gold coins to be given away at her engagement party had almost been collected by Pighi who, moreover, had her dowry almost ready. But Manolis no longer wanted to hear anything about this match.

"Me go into the Thomases' house again and talk to Stratis? This can't be done, so get it out of your mind," he said, straight out.

"Very well," Saitonicolis said, "when the time comes we'll discuss it again. Only don't forget that I want to make Pighi my daughter-in-law."

In the meanwhile Tereres took courage and renewed his overtures to Thomas. Pighi revealed to Saitonicolis in despair that her brother was pressing her to accept. And because, she declared that either she would marry Manolis or nobody, Stratis started to beat her up and it was with difficulty that Thomas saved her from his wrath.

In addition, Reginio attempted to rekindle and take advantage of her son's hatred for Tereres and Stratis in order to arouse his sympathy for Pighi. She told him about all the poor girl had suffered on his behalf. Saitonicolina's words were not entirely without result. Manolis became thoughtful and whispered threats against Tereres and Stratis. But then, with a violent jerk, as if he were shaking off some oppressive burden, he said?

"Let Tereres and even the devil marry her, the moustachioed one! It's her fault, all of it. She's no better than her brother. This head of lettuce is from the same garden."

And, according to a habit which he had latterly acquired, he stopped the conversation abruptly and went out, not wanting to hear any more.

Saitonicolis began to fear that he had loosened the reins too much for him and now it would be difficult to draw them in. Donkeys, he said, should not be given very much initiative because they begin to think they are the riders. Again he listened to his wife who advised moderation, saying more bread is eaten with honey than with vinegar. To help the mother, all the relatives came and advised Manolis. But all that honey was spread in vain. Manolis preferred the sour grape and remained unconvinced. Nevertheless, he thought to take advantage of his father's yielding nature and asked a favor, to which Saitonicolis consented, hoping that this would contribute to bringing the apostate back in line.

Marghi, it seems, finally realizing that Smyrnios was not as shrewd in love as she supposed him to be, decided to liberate her secret from the depths of her heart. So she confessed to her friends her feelings towards the owner of the coffee-shop. This, having been announced, reached Manolis too, who innocently assumed that Marghi preferred Smyrnios because of his occupation. Therefore, in order to neutralize his rival's advantage and to raise himself in

Zervodhopoula's esteem, it would be necessary for him to open a store too. Saitonicolis joined him in his wish in the hope that the new occupation would contribute to his becoming reasonable and not leave him time for mischief. The first floor of his house was already complete and this was allocated, temporarily, for the commercial venture. But Manolis, taking possession of the house, had another motive, since he anticipated that his father's patience and tractability would not last long. Saitonicolis, gave his consent with his own goal in mind, only on one condition: that the coffee-shop be open only on holidays, while on the rest of the days Manolis would help with the agricultural tasks.

Manolis' first customers were Astronomos, who volunteered to guide and help him in his work, and Barbarezos, who volunteered, no less willingly to help Manolis in the area of consumption, drinking coffee and smoking hookahs without paying. From the first day the inn-keeper suffered significant losses. Wanting to imitate the playful agility and rapidity with which Smyrnios washed the hookahs, he broke two of the five he had in the shop. Barbarezos, forestalling any possible negative explanation, shouted, "good luck!" and asked for another coffee.

One of Manolis' first considerations was to make known to the daughter of the widow his change in situation, since, because of it, he had become a coffee-house keeper. Girded, therefore, with a colored towel for an apron, he passed in front of Zervoudhena's house, and, when he saw Marghi, he shouted to her:

"Ay . . .! What do you have to say about this, Marouli? Smyrnios isn't the only coffee-house keeper; there's another."

"Well, well, look who's mixing with people. Oh! Get lost!"

With a quick movement she turned her back to him and closed herself in the house while Manolis stood in the road completely confused. He had pinned such hopes on the impression that apron would make; now he was quite upset. He would have given up hope completely, if the widow had not enheartened him with convincing and encouraging words to persist. What? Would a young brute of a man like himself, allow Smyrnios, a runt of a man, to take the girl from him?

Thus, Manolis began thinking that the only obstacle to his desires was Yianakos and his spite turned toward him, and shortly thereafter was transformed into mortal hatred. When, therefore, in his frenzied outbursts, he stabbed his dagger into the trees shouted to the widow's daughter:

"This is how I'll nail that dog Smyrnios!"

One evening, while Yianakos was going home to sleep, in the darkness he made out the shape of a man lying in wait at a corner. That man jumped up suddenly, revealing his gigantic stature, and rushed toward him shouting:

"How can I let you live any longer!"

Smyrnios recognized Patouchas, and, in a flash, he thwarted Manolis by throwing his overcoat in his face; taking advantage of Manolis' momentary confusion, he gave him a kick in the legs which overturned him. In a few seconds Manolis had been knocked over, disarmed, and felt Smyrnios' knee on his chest and the edge of his own knife at his neck.

"I'll teach you how to kill," Yianakos was telling him, gasping.

"Do whatever you want," Manolis said, completely disheartened.

"I don't kill Christians," Smyrnios said almost sweetly, "and, besides, you're the son of my best friend. I just want you to tell me what you have against me."

"I don't have anything against you, only you love the Zervodopoula and she doesn't want me," Manolis said like a child complaining. "I was a bit drunk, too."

Yianakos laughed and let him get up.

"And who told you that I love her?"

"She says so."

"It's not true, Manolis. I give her to you, my friend, and I hope you enjoy her."

"Is that true?" Manolis said, with childish joy.

"It's true, and the next time don't believe whatever you're told."

Handing over the dagger to Manolis, he wished him goodnight and went away calmly, as if nothing had happened.

"How the devil did he put me down and take my knife!" Manolis was thinking in admiration. "And how strong his hands are! They gripped me like iron."

Manolis emerged from that incident rather pleased. What was he after? To get rid of a rival? He succeeded in what he wanted without unpleasant complications with the Moudir and the gendarmes, whom the wine made him overlook. In fact, since Smyrnios told him that he could have Zervodhopoula, he believed that he had given her to him. As for his shame, it was concealed by the darkness of the night. The important thing was that Marouli was now his. With this conviction he said to himself:

"And now how are you going to get away from me? Where are you going to go, Marouli?"

With the help of his drunkenness, which had not completely dissipated, his thought reached such enthusiasm, that he soon began to sing softly:

> And now, my Marouli, how are you
> going to get away from me?
> Willing or not, you will love me.

But his new hopes, too, dissolved at his first encounter with the widow's daughter. He saw her at the window, and having again received her rude gestures in response to his flirtatious words, he said to her:

"Whatever you do, you're going to fall into my hands. I'll make you mine. Smyrnios doesn't want you, so put it out of your mind."

Marghi's blush turned completely white. And Manolis continued:

"He himself told me last night."

Now, instead of seeing her falling at his feet, as he had imagined, he saw a flower pot coming down on him.

Along with the flower pot a stream of abuse came from the window.

"Better if your eyes fall out, you ugly creature! Even if you and I alone were left in the world, I wouldn't want you."

Manolis, leaping back just in time, calmly gave a beautiful answer:

"But if I had a thousand girls to choose from, I'd pick you."

And then:

"Curse me, shame me, thumb your nose at me, throw flower pots at me, hit me, kill me, but I won't become angry."

This was a new type of stubbornness for him not to become angry. Whenever his patience was in danger of being exhausted, the widow would appear and persuade him to keep on trying to ripen the sour grape and reinforced his flagging hopes. His women relatives began to suspect that Zervoudhena had used witchcraft on him, that she had given him something to drink which made him crazy. What could they tell her? The widow could turn their accusations against them, since her daughter did not want him and he insisted on bothering and chasing her. However, they knew that Kalio sought out Manolis almost every day to pick his brain.

Although he wanted to appear as if he did not attach any importance to his son's love for Zervodhopoula, Saitonicolis was seriously worried. Especially when the appointed time for his engagement and marriage to Pighi approached, he continued to show total indifference. One day he said:

"But, what the devil, is the widow's little chick made of honey so he can't give her up after all the insults she's heaped on him? That unfortunate Pighi didn't do a thing to him: she loves him to distraction and he doesn't even have eyes to see her. I can't understand what kind of a person he is."

Thus he decided to put an end to this situation.

"Manolis," he told him one evening with calm severity, "the time for your engagement to Pighi is near, but you have to control yourself. All green young men have wild oats to sow, but you've overdone it. I don't want you to talk to the Zervodhopoula again or else we'll be at each other's throats."

Manolis looked at him with impertinent calm.

"You're wasting your words," he said. "How many times do you want me to tell you that I don't want Pighi even if they cover her with gold. I want Zervodhopoula, and it's Zervodhopoula I'll marry."

Saitonicolis was astounded because he wasn't expecting such insolence.

"Say that again, buster! Say what you said again!" he said, half standing and trembling from restrained anger.

"I'm saying it and I'll say it again. It's Zervodhopoula I'm . . ."

But Saitonicolis did not let him complete his sentence. He leapt enraged. And, seizing a thick piece of wood, he dashed at him. Reginio managed to place herself between them just in time, and crying, she threw herself on her husband's neck and implored him not to heed Manolis' words.

Manolis having gotten up and headed to the door, said:

"I'm not marrying that moustachioed girl and you can do whatever you want."

"Out, out of my house, you scum," Saitonicolis roared, beside himself with anger.

Trying to break away from his wife's arms whose strength was multiplied tenfold by motherly love, he continued:

"Out! Don't let my eyes see you again. I don't want to know you."

Manolis hit his fists against each other.

"Zervodhopoula, Zervodhopoula, Zervodhopoula is the one I'm going to marry."

And he started to leave. But Saitonicolis, pushing away his wife, overtook him before he had crossed the threshold and gave him a hard whack. Reginio again managed to restrain him in time and cried, "In God's name, Nikolio, it's your child you're going to kill!" And so she gave Manolis time to save himself from the paternal wrath.

Manolis took refuge in his coffe-shop in order to sleep there. He no longer had a place at home. That was something he had to accept.

He met the widow next day and told her what had happened. But while he expected consolation and hope, Kalio had changed her tune. What would happen now that Marghi remained unconvinced? Until then, she had hoped that she could change her mind, finally she had realized that it was impossible, absolutely impossible.

"She doesn't want you, doesn't want you, doesn't want you. She chokes, beats herself, because she doesn't want you. And what shall I do to her? I did what I could."

"And what about the sour grape you were telling me about?"

"That's what I believed, but since she's as stubborn as an Arab, what would you have me do?"

Manolis sighed.

"And now?" he said dolefully.

The widow appeared to hesitate, then stammering she said.

"I think you should leave both of them; Marghi and Pighi . . . They're both frivolous girls, still brainless. And make up your mind . . . and marry a quiet woman . . . a prudent one . . . . Such a woman suits you."

But the only thing he understood of the widow's words was that she was advising him to give up her daughter. Then stubbornly, he said:

"I'm going to marry her, whether she wants me or not."

8

Manolis' distress at his expulsion did not last long. When the first impact was over and he was able to think more coolly, being alone in his home, which was already complete in everything save the housewife whom it awaited, he felt the relief of a slave who regains his freedom. He no longer had anyone on his back and he could live however he wished and marry whenever and however he wanted. Thus, he was free of the endless tasks which his father assigned him and free to follow the promptings of his madness, which circulated with the overheated blood in his veins. The joy which he felt imagining that free and unbridled life also mitigated the bitterness left in his soul by the widow's disheartening words. In any case, at the last moment, he had found a way out of his impasse.

"She won't do it willingly?" he thought, "I'll take her by force; I'll abduct her."

The idea of abduction was fixed in his mind, from that moment on. Anyway, it was not a difficult matter. Zervodopoula was not muscular like Pighi for him to fear her resistance. She was so small that he would lift her up like a child and in two jumps he would arrive home. And, afterwards, Saitonicolis could shout as much as he wanted for him to marry Pighi. The whole affair seemed so easy to him that, as he thought about it, he imagined it an accomplished fact, and the widow's delicate daughter quivering in his embrace. Indeed this imagined emotion of his was so vivid that it overflowed in sensual shudders in his nerves.

The execution of his decision was postponed by the willfulness which the persistent and invincible aversion of Marghi roused in his soul. He was made stubborn by the idea that, after so many efforts, he had not managed to hear a kind word from her lips. His manly pride revolted. Was he so ugly and stupid that after so much effort he was not able to have his way with a girl? And because the widow's axiom about the sour grape established itself in his brain like an absolute truth, he was made even more stubborn, realizing, or rather seeing, that through him it was being disproved, and the sour grape, instead of becoming sweeter with time, was becoming even more sour. Was it possible that he was repulsive and incapable of inspiring love in a woman? The widow had an opposing opinion. After all, how was it possible for Pighi to love him? Therefore, it was not

144

impossible for him to be loved by Zervodhopoula too, and, moreover, his sense of honor compelled him to persist in order to silence those who had begun to make fun of him for his failures and whispered to him as he passed by, "she doesn't want you." If he again failed, he now knew what he would do.

He renewed his armorous siege with greater fervor and force. But Marghi's resistance and dislike increased accordingly. In fact, from the day he told her that Smyrnios did not love her, her hatred, instead of decreasing, expressed itself in a more savage and unrelenting manner. The conviction that Smyrnios could love and choose only her for a wife was so strongly rooted in her heart that, even if Yianakos himself told her he did not love her, she would not have believed it. The worst she could conjecture was that Patouchas' antics might have cooled Smyrnios' secret love. But this was even one more reason to hate him the more and for her to show her aversion more strongly. In her persistent dislike for him she found unexpected encouragement.

Her mother now recognized that Manolis, whom she too began to call Patouchas, was not suitable for her.

"You're right, my child. Such a man is not for you. You're right and I was wrong."

In a similar manner, at every meeting with Manolis she systematically strove to convince him that he should not persist in his efforts to get her daughter.

"Even if you marry her, what'll you do with her since she doesn't want you? You'll pass all your life nagging and quarreling. I, too, wanted you to marry her and I spoke to her and tried to persuade her a thousand times. But since she doesn't want you, I can't put a rope around her neck. Besides, on my word, a wife like Marghi or Pighi is not suitable for you. They're still little girls and can't distinguish the good from bad. Nor do they know how to love and adore the man they marry. Their brains haven't set yet. The best thing is for you to let them be foolish and look for a prudent woman . . . a woman who'd love you and whom you'd love. And, in the last analysis, it's not appropriate for you to beg. They should beg you."

And each time she seemed to have something more to say, but it was difficult for her and she hesitated to utter it. Manolis did not see anything irregular in this transformation of the widow. It seemed to him the result of her daugher's obstinate resistance. Her advice was sufficiently vague for its real meaning to escape him. In any case, he had already made his decision and considered it a matter of honor to resolve the matter. Marghi would become his by hook or crook.

Easter came and went, and month after month went by, and Manolis remained incorrigible. Saitonicolis, too, remained unshakable in his decision. Now he was saying that he would disown and disinherit his son if he married a girl other than Pighi.

"For me," he would say, "Pighi is my child. If he marries her, he'll also be my child, and if he doesn't marry her, only Pighi will be my child and she'll receive his share of my wealth."

He repeated this to Thomas, who had begun to fret.

"Don't take what's his name seriously, Koubare. I gave you my word and I'll keep my word. I told you that Pighi would be my child? She will. If Manolis marries her they'll both be my children. If he marries another, Pighi will be my child and he the disinherited one."

"We don't want charity," Thomas murmured, "only try to straighten out your fine-feathered son because he's become insufferable."

"What'll I do to him? Shall I kill him? I did whatever I could and now I've left it to God to enlighten him."

However, he also permitted his wife to look after the apostate, and he pretended neither to know nor to care how Manolis was fed and clothed. Reginio would not stop giving advice to Manolis and trying to arouse him on behalf of Pighi. But she was wasting her words.

"If you're coming to talk to me about the moustachioed one," Manolis would say angrily, "don't come."

"But, my dear child, don't you feel sorry for the unfortunate girl who's became flesh and bones because of the love she has for you?"

"I don't feel sorry for anyone!"

A few days later, though, when he accidentally saw Pighi at the fountain, he was not able to remain indifferent; something not unlike a twinge of conscience disturbed his soul. Poor Pighi was so miserable. Of the formerly fresh, cheerful and vivacious maiden, there remained only a melancholy shadow. But such feelings could not stay long in the heart of a drunkard like Manolis. A little later, all that remained of his impression was that, because of her thinnness, the down over Pighi's mouth was more obvious now, a true moustache. And he expelled the memory of the fountain with a gesture.

"Go to the devil, moustachioed one!"

Having exhausted all his means of mollifying the widow's daughter, he thought of trying exhibitions of strength and bravery. And when he saw her, he pulled up the wide sleeve of his silk shirt in order to display his herculean arm. Dashing onto the rooftops, he would shout:

"Only brave men can fight for Sfakia!"

Lifting up huge stones, he carried them and placed them before Zervodhopoula, as a tribute of strength to beauty. Then Marghi deigned to smile mockingly. But Manolis, taking these smiles as rays of a rising love, was encouraged to even more daring feats of this kind. One day, when he saw Zervodhopoula returning from the fair at Aghia Moni, he thought of lifting her, along with the donkey on which she was sitting, to his shoulders and carry her in this manner to her door. He acted instantly on his idea, but the terrified Marghi jumped off the donkey in time. Manolis who had already put himself under the donkey, lifted it alone and so he carried it triumphantly to the widow's house.

These feats, aside from the fact that their results were no different from his previous efforts, began to arouse a general outcry against him. The scandal exceeded all limits. Never before had such things happened in the village. And since Zervodhopoula did not have a father, or a brother, nor any other relatives to defend her, the villagers thought that they had an obligation to protect her and the decorum of their customs. Therefore, on Sunday, after the liturgy had ended, there was a lively discussion outside Aghia Aekaterini, in the presence of Saitonicolis, who listened sadly in silence and appeared to be extremely weary. Finally, he said:

"I did what I could. My tongue has grown hair on it from talking to him. When I saw that he wouldn't listen, I threw him out of my house and it's almost a year since then. And now with this affliction he's caused me, if I start talking to him and he talks back at me, I'll kill him, but I don't want to commit such a great sin. You, my fellow villagers, do whatever you want. The wisest of you take him aside and talk to him, threaten him with the Moudir; and if he doesn't listen, I don't care if you even kill him. You have every right because it's true that such things have never happened in our village."

If Saitonicolis had not enjoyed the general respect and love of his fellow villagers, that uprising would have taken place a long time ago. Even now, his words moderated the indignation of those who gathered together outside the church, and grieved those who found themselves obliged to cause him bitterness. Nevertheless the elders did not neglect to speak quite severely to Manolis and to threaten that if he did not straighten himself out they would ask for the assistance of the Moudir and the gendarmes.

Even Zervoudhena had complained to the elders. Manolis' recent antics angered her terribly. Her daughter's tears, after the incident with the donkey, completely shook up her motherly affection. She was an honorable woman and her intentions were by no means unholy. These doings jeopardized her daughter and gave people a reason to laugh at them both. She decided to find Manolis herself and talk to him candidly. Since they had told him again and again that they did not want him, he should be ashamed and leave her daughter alone unless he was as shameless and unfeeling as a pig. But when she confronted Manolis her wrath subsided. This is what happened every time. How could she be angry with this person? Instead of rebuking him in accordance with her decision threatening that she would go to the bishop and to the Moudir, and rend her clothes,[58] she talked to him gently and with a maternal complaint. Gradually she came to the usual advice that he should marry a wise woman. But when she arrived at that point, her tongue faltered again.

She repeated herself and fell into confusion. She saw that Manolis did not understand her and she wanted to say something else, but this something else was too weighty and large for her tongue, despite its agility, to push it between the lips. And her suffering was great. Manolis, still not realizing that the widow was waiting to be understood without expressing herself, said:

"The most prudent woman in the world is Marouli and I'm going to marry her whether she wants it ot not."

The widow sighed. She was suffering terribly. The agonizing battle which was taking place in her heart was rattling her judgement. She tried again, but once again her tongue struck an insuperable barrier. Then she said one thing for another, as though dizzy, and at one point her eyes became blank, and at another, they emitted feverish sparks. But Manolis neither guessed, nor saw anything of that tempest. Moreover, he had his own private tempest. He had finally completely given up hope in his amorous undertakings. And before him appeared as unavoidable now the second part of his decision: the abduction. After he had thought a little , he said to the widow:

"Tell your daughter that I'm going to abduct her. I'm sick and tired of this."

The widow sighed again; she stood there, watching him as he went away, until he was out of sight.

Manolis proceeded pensively. Suddenly he jumped up, hearing the voice of a child coming from a nearby rooftop:

"She doesn't want you, Manolis."

He turned with fury, but the demon-child was not in sight. He continued his way, but after a little that same voice made him turn with even greater fury.

"She doesn't want you, Patouchas, she doesn't want you!"

And like an echo, another child's voice added:

"She'd prefer red shoes!"

Manolis turned around with savage looks, but the children had hidden or run off and he did not see anyone. The nickname bothered him little now; he had become accustomed to it the way a person becomes accustomed to a chronic ailment. In addition, so many others in the village had a derisive nickname side by side with their real one. He was not alone. But that phrase gave him the impression of being slapped. It was not enough that Zervodhopoula said it to him ten times a day, but it was necessary for others to repeat it to him, too, even the children from the rooftops.

He cursed and went away, but the voices of the children pursued him:

"She doesn't want you! She doesn't want you!"

"She doesn't want me," murmured Manolis raging. "I know she doesn't want me, but I'm going to make her want me. Just good-bye for now."

He was so shaken that without being aware of it he entered the street which passed before Thomas' house. A whole year had gone by since he had passed by on that street. He knew, though, that the sound of the loom, which then used to move him so, had become silent and the flowers in the window had been neglected, while a veil of gloom covered that house which once was made cheerful by Pighi's graceful countenance. One might have thought that the horrible fez of the stern old man had extended throughout that home and strangled every joy. In any case, Pighi rarely appeared there. She accompanied and helped her brother with the farm tasks where she was baked all day beneath the sun and was lashed by the rain and sometimes by Stratis.

When Manolis realized his mistake, it was already too late. He was very close to Thomas' house and among the branches of the mulberry-tree, he discerned Pighi just as he had seen her once standing at the door scattering barley to the hens. Its was also the same hour. But now the rosy light of the afternoon framed a most miserable picture. How the poor girl had changed. She was unrecognizable! When she saw him and turned her eyes to him,

Manolis felt something of the excitement which those sweet black eyes formerly gave him. But he immediately shook off that feeling and turned his eyes away with an angry gesture:

"Go to the devil, moustachioed one!"

And he went by without seeing Thomas, who, sitting by the door, with one foot unshod, was busy pulling his boot.

"The fine-feathered . . .," he grunted upon seeing Manolis.

For some time after the menacing hints of the elders, Manolis seemed to have become reasonable, but not so much out of fear, as out of necessity. He was no longer afraid. Astronomos once said about him that if the ox knew its strength it would tear the world to pieces. So now the ox had come to know its strength; while, on one hand, it was not tearing up the world, on the other, it no longer feared it.

Manolis appeared to be good because the unlucky Zervodhopoula, learning of his threats, had stopped going out. But if he did not see the daughter, he saw the mother daily. Every day the widow had to endure the torment of wanting to utter the secret which burned her heart. Now and then she just dared, while speaking to him, to rub, like a cat, against his clothing, but immediately she would pull back agitated, as though she had touched a flame. The trembling of her eyes, her face now pallid now red, her quivering lips and the agonized heaving of her chest revealed more eloquently what her voice did not dare to utter. But Manolis did not guess a thing. He arrived a stone and a stone he was leaving. How could he guess something which he was incapable of imagining? There were moments when the widow trembled in fear that Manolis might guess that which she concealed in her heart. The miserable woman suffered between two conflicting inclinations as she had never suffered during her long widowhood. As white hair had begun to appear on her head and wrinkles furrowed her brow, these harbingers of old age exacerbated her natural terror of aging and she grew still more nervous and feverish, hoping Manolis would guess the cause of her distress. To that pressure other thoughts raised insurmountable obstacles. "Aren't you ashamed," an austere inner voice said to her, "you who have a marriageable daughter . . .? Aren't you ashamed? What will the village say?" She would then fall into a bitter depression and, sighing would say:

"My God, come down and take me so I can be saved . . . so my senses won't leave my head."

Indeed, her mind, which had never enjoyed complete equilibrium, had suffered serious impairment. Occasionally while speaking, she would stop in the middle of a sentence, and possessed by absent-mindedness, she would forget the rest or she repeated what she had said before. While walking in the street she would talk to herself and her distraction was so great, that often she followed a road which took her away from the very place to which she was going. Often she would become furious, without any special reason and without apparent provocation from her daughter. Then, almost immediately, her anger would cease and she would become excessively affectionate and caressing. Occasionally, during such moments of regret, she cried and reproved herself as a cross and unjust mother.

Even in that agitation of her reason she neither forgot nor neglected to take certain precautions: her cunning was maintained undiminished. Fearing the suspicions and the gossip which could be aroused by her frequent meetings and secret conversations with Manolis, she would say, as though indignant, whenever they saw her leaving him:

"He doesn't listen, he doesn't listen . . . It's a hopeless task talking to that fellow. My tongue has dried up telling him he's wasting his time, but he sticks to his tune. Why don't those he belongs to gather him up."

Thus, she also silenced Saitonicolis who was often suspicious of the frequent meetings between the "mad one" and his "crazy one." Whenever he tried to reproach her, the widow responded indignantly. It was not enough that her daughter and she were in trouble because of the son; now they had to suffer from the father's words as well. So she was supposed to let his impudent son make her daughter a laughing stock, and she, not talk to him. What breeding!

In effect, she was not a little distressed at her daughter's position from fear of Patouchas. Marghi no longer even dared go to church. How long could this situation last? Marghi cried night and day. Her despair reached a peak when she was invited to a dance, and she did not dare go even though she loved dancing and, indeed, she sang and danced admirably.

But at the dance something happened which would put an end to the state of seige in which she lived. The dance took place on the eve of a holiday at the upper end of the village, and brought together most of the young men and girls of the village in one of the most spacious houses. Besides Marghi, Pighi was also absent. What did that terribly unhappy girl want amidst such joy?

The dance floor was spacious; yet many young people were sitting and standing around, waiting their turn. But they participated in the singing by repeating after the dancers the *mattinada,* which was first spoken by the person dancing at the head of the line and to which they answered with a second couplet.

Alexandris, the blind lyrist,[59] sitting in the middle of the dancers, appeared to be under the spell of his own music. He moved his head to left and right, as if he were chasing flies, and he smiled the cold half-smile of a blind person, from which the radiance of the eyes is missing. With the movement of his bow the sounds of the *pidhiktos*[60] became still more lively. And the whole circle of dancers moved as one.

The sound of feet echoed together so loudly one thought the ground was shaking. There were moments when the lyre positively barked, as they say, while the dancing became frenzied. Then the dancers seemed to grow into giants whose heads almost touched the ceiling. The daggers shook in the belts of the young men, and the breasts of the female dancers trembled and throbbed under the silk bodices.

In the meantime couplets crossed back and forth like arrows with the fast pace of the dance; at times, they consisted of amatory or taunting dialogue. Sometimes the leader of the dance would sing a couplet first; at others one of the dancers or one of those standing outside the circle of the dance, and all of the dancers would then repeat them. The exchange of taunting couplets was mostly improvisation. Some exhibited the poetic treasures of their memory, and, in responding to other mattinadas they began with the word with which the previous couplet ended. Then the stychomythia was followed and enriched by passionate selections from *Erotokritos,* especially Arethousa's farewell.

Manolis was there. Leaning on a window he seemed thoughtful and melancholy. Zervodopoula had not come to the dance, evidently to avoid meeting him. This gave him one more reason to think that her resistance was impossible to overcome except by force, by abduction. But now, since she stopped going out, even abduction became difficult. Moreover, even if he tried to grab her in the road, there was the danger that the villagers would catch up with him and take her out of his hands. The safest thing would be to abduct her some night from her home, to open or break down the door and seize her.

The *pidhiktos* was followed by the quiet, undulating and restful *sighanos*[61] whose slow, loose rhythm allowed the dancers to sing drawn out songs. A pretty, young married woman at the front of the line began to sing one of the commonest songs of the sighanos.

A young lass went with her lad to see him off to sea.
Holding a candle to light his way,
a glass to give him drink
with each glass, with every smile,
she says another word.
You're leaving, my Constantine,
and what will you bring back to me . . . .

And every hemistich was repeated by all the dancers. The dancers, having sung many contemporary tunes, stopped so they could rest and the lyrist could tune his lyre and rub his bow with resin for another *pidhiktos*.

Various people repeatedly invited Manolis to dance, but he did not accept, saying that he was not in the mood. The truth is that he did not have any confidence in his ability as a dancer. Even though he tried very hard to learn, his movements were still so unpolished and stiff that it was said he danced "as if he were putting straw in a sack." He felt all eyes were mockingly directed at his feet, and this brought confusion to his lower extremities as though the huge feet themselves had feelings and a sense of honor. But when the *pidhiktos* was repeated, he saw Tereres standing by the fireplace and answering the couplets of the young man dancing at the head of the line, Manolis thought he should dance in order to counterbalance the enemy's display by means of another display. He did not know how to sing, but Tereres did not know how to dance. So after a few turns of the *pidhiktos*, he pulled his wide sleeves up to the shoulder, as he did whenever he was inspired by his madness and went to the head of the line.

His appearance at the head of the line cheered up almost all the faces; Astronomos, who was among the spectators, called to the blind lyrist:

"Your most powerful bow strokes, Alexandris! You know who's at the head of the line?"

The blind man's face became calmer, while his head nodded that he had guessed. He had already heard the stamp of a foot which had shaken the ground, and this alone was enough for him to understand that Manolis was leading the dance.

"We wish you a long life, lion of our village!" he shouted to Manolis and his bow became livelier.

Even those who were most disposed to laugh at Manolis were

forced to acknowledge that he presented a spectacle of exceptional strength and robustness. They all said, "Just wait and see what a man he will be. Without his boorishness, he could become one of the handsomest young men of the village."

"Faster!" shouted Manolis, entering the spirit of the dance.

While the lyre played the fastest turns of the *pidhiktos,* Manolis was jumping to great heights. And while he was in the air, he would hit first one leg and then the other with the palm of his hand. Then he would bend back his body or, bending his knees, would spring up with astonishing elasticity. Sometimes, he would sigh and, at others, let out whoops of excitement. Alexandris seemed to be struggling to wear him out and played quickly, almost continuously. Manolis not only was not getting tired, he was becoming even more spirited: after a while, he started emphasizing the rhythm with whistles so piercing and loud that the women covered their ears.

In the midst of his enthusiasm he spotted Tereres and, as he went back and forth, gave him secret glances and was ready, it seemed, to kick him too, in time with the rhythm of the *pidhiktos.* Also, perhaps because of Tereres, he decided after the previous display, to show off his voice. But the number of the couplets he knew was very limited and he was obliged to repeat them. Tereres, whose maliciousness was so great it overcame his fear, availed himself of the opportunity to tease him. His voice was heard directing a mocking shaft at Manolis:

> You shouldn't repeat the same mattinada
> Cause the girls'll think you don't know anotha.

Manolis' nostrils flared from angry breath and his eyes turned a savage glare toward the fireplace where the enemy was standing. For a moment he thought of leaving the dance and grabbing him by the neck. But, then, it occurred to him that it was necessary to answer by way of a couplet in order to show that he was not the beast Tereres wanted to make him out to be. So with great effort he managed to improvise a response which he punctuated with a terrible stamping of the foot:

> Hang on to your mattinadas, say them nigh-nigh
> I'll bind you like a goat and hang you very high.

In order to make up his couplet Manolis was forced to make up a word, the adverb "nigh-nigh." Here he made a start which in the future would assume the dimensions with which we are familiar today in poetry and in prose.

The answer was received with laughter, because the binding and hanging up of Tereres were common knowledge, as were the latter's threats which had provoked that revenge. Manolis was pleased with the impression his couplet made. His anger ended, and he too laughed with the others. But, as the dancers passed by Tereres, Manolis turned toward him with a threatening gesture and shouted as would a child:

"Boo!"

Manolis' game sparked and renewed the boisterious laughter of the crowd and the trembling of Tereres who had become livid.

"Now, would a murderer be blamed?" he said, leaning towards Astronomos who was sitting near him.

"Look, friend, stop talking like this," Nikolakis said to him, "because if he hears you, he'll attack you, and all of us together won't be able to save you from his hands. He's a giant; can't you see?"

Manolis, encouraged by his first success, was occupied with a new improvisation, as he continued dancing. The poetic contest would have ended, it seems, in a very unpleasant manner for the mandrake, if something else had not appeared to attract the attention of Manolis and the others.

Five Turks, known palikaria who often sought fights with Christians, had entered shortly before. Because of the noise and jostling of the dancing, very few had seen them during the first moments they were there. The Turks stood near the entrance and seemed to be waiting to be offered seats. But when those dancing and those standing around the dancers saw them, their faces darkened. Whispers were heard, while the younger people directed glances of surprise and annoyance toward the Turks. The Turks, though, maintained an insolent indifference and, as if ignoring the expressions of hostility which they saw around them, they showed intentions of taking part in the dancing.

After a while however, the elder Aeras, approached them, and after saying good-evening, he said to them:

"Won't you tell me, my little aghas, why did you come here?"

"We came to dance," one of the Turks answered.

"I don't believe you came here to dance. Here there are only Christians with their wives and sisters. If you had come to dance, you would have brought along your sisters and your wives."

"What, us bring along our women so that they could dance with Greeks?" said the Turk, approaching Aeras menacingly.

The *pidhikos* automatically changed to a *sighanos* and the blind man's bow barely touched the strings. A silence similar to the calm before a storm held for a few moments, and all eyes were fixed upon the Turks and the elder who said:

"Since it's not right for your women to dance with Greeks, how can it be right for our women to dance with Turks?"

"Cut the talk," another Turk said, "now that we're here we're going to dance."

And he made as if to push Aeras aside and go forward to the circle of the dancers. But the elder grabbed him by the arm with a sturdy hand and said emphatically:

"The time of the janissaries[62] is over, son. And whoever wants to act like a janissary is going to get clobbered."

"No, it's not over, you icon-worshipper, and you'll see," the Turk said, pushing the elder roughly.

The Turks put their hands on their daggers, but several young men dashed at them at once.

"The dancing will not stop!" Patouchas shouted and, raising a heavy chair, like a club, he threw himself into the brawl.

The Turks' resistance lasted only briefly. The most impudent of them, known as Sabris, fell in the doorway with his skull cracked by a blow from Patouchas. Under blows from rods and chairs, the daggers fell from their hands and the Turks sought refuge in flight. Manolis and the other young men chased them as far as the Turkish quarters, where the other Turks who ran to their aid suffered the same fate, or even worse, in order to learn that the time of the janissaries was over . . . .

The next day, when Manolis woke up at his sister's, where he had slept, he learned two pleasant things: that his conduct during the fight with the Turks had elated the villagers, and that Smyrnios had become engaged to Symvoulos' daughter. What would Zervodopoula say now? Would she still insist on refusing him now that, on one hand, she had no hope for Smyrnios, and, on the other, Manolis was swathed in heroic brilliance?

Soon he was heading toward Zervodopoula's house, happy and singing. But on the way he heard someone call him and turning around saw Spyridolenia. On that day the face of the nit-picker did not have its usual mocking expression.

"Manolio," she said to him, "I want to kiss the hand that broke Sabris' head last night. But go away, my child, go away because I found out that the Turkish gendarmes are looking for you. Go away quickly!"

156

Manolis was troubled, but then he said stubbornly:

"Let them come near me. I'm not going anywhere."

And he went on his way. He had not gone far when he saw an Albanian-Turk gendarme coming from the opposite direction. He turned back in order to flee, but he saw another coming from that direction. The latter shouted to him:

"Stop, Patouchas!"

Manolis stopped because he saw there was no way out, while the Turkish gendarmes coming near seized him by the arms.

"What do you want from me?" Manolis asked.

"You'll find out later. Once you're in the lock-up you'll find out."

"You're going to put me in the lock-up?" Manolis said, as he finally began to realize the seriousness of the situation.

He had horrible ideas about jail, because he heard that the prisoners were bound hand and foot with heavy chains and whipped almost every day, or that others died in prison, while still others came out with their health completely destroyed. But the idea alone that he would lose his freedom, and along with it Zervodopoula, now that he was almost certain of her consent, brought him to despair. The thought of such danger gave him the strength to shake off the gendarmes and, with two kicks, to knock both of them to the ground. Then he turned to flight. But when he reached the corner of the road, he turned a moment towards the Albanians and shaking his upraised forearm, he shouted at them, trying to imitate their pronunciation:

"Nia, you scald-heads!"

How could the Albanians catch him now? He ran with the speed of a chamois. Nevertheless, he did not miss passing by Zervoudhena's street. There he slowed his pace. The widow was standing at the door; Marghi was sitting inside, her eyes red from crying.

"I'm leaving because the Albanians are after me," Manolis said to the mother. "But just have Marouli wait for me. I'll come and get her after a short while."

And he departed for the mountains without hearing Marghi's answer:

"Better that your eyes fall out instead!"

9

It was the last Sunday of the Pre-Lenten Festival[63] and from the Christian quarters of the village came the sound of general merriment. People were dancing in various houses and, in the churchyards and at the crossroads, young men and children were bowling and playing different athletic games. Only Patouchas' noisy liveliness was missing from those groups of young men because Manolis and two of the young men were still fleeing justice, being pursued for the fight at the dance. Three other young men, not escaping in time, had been arrested and sent to prison at Kastro. The three fugitives met and went about together, receiving hospitality from the shepherds, who gave them every comfort and informed or hid them whenever the gendarmes came out in pursuit of them.

For a few days it had been rumored that the Moudir, giving in to Smyrnios' efforts and Saitonicolis' gifts, had promised to give up the chase. The Turks, however, pressured him, saying that for the peace of the village, Patouchas should not be temporarily imprisoned, but exiled to the Barbary Coast.

Saitonicolis himself was so pleased with Manolis' brave action that he forgave him.

"May he have my blessing," he said. "He lifted all the heavy-heartedness from my heart at once."

"See that, and you thought he was a coward?" Reginio said to him.

"He was a bit, but it was from inexperience. He was still a boy, to tell the truth. It doesn't matter, all's well that ends well. But did you hear how he dusted off the Albanians and escaped from their hands? Spyridolenia was there and she tells about it. I had sworn to pull her tongue out with the cloth from the priest's cassock, because I learned she was the one who made up the nickname, but since I heard of her praises, I started liking her. The Turks are ready to drink poison and Sabris confesses that he has never seen such a powerful man."

"And the Moudir?" Reginio said anxiously.

"The Moudir threatens, but what can he do? Those Albanians can't catch Manolis easily, even if a hundred of them go after him. I'll send him the rifle and order him to trade fire for fire. It's better if you're the mother of a murderer than of a dead man."

"And you should have seen poor Pighi, how happy she was!"

Saitonicolina said after a short silence. "It's been a long time since I've seen her laugh."

"And Thomas, too, did you forget . . .? Our in-law is delighted. Even Stratis. Would you believe that Stratis would ever say something good about Manolis?"

Occasionally Manolis came down to make a secret visit to the village, but he never went to his father's home. Saitonicolis had informed him that he had forgiven him for the past, but always under the condition that he marry Pighi. But Manolis answered that only Zervodhopoula would be his wife. And whenever he came down to the village he never missed passing by Zervoudhena's house. But Marghi continued to avoid him with undiminished aversion. Neither his glory nor Smyrnios' engagement had changed the situation. On the contrary, Marghi ascribed to him the responsibility for Yianakos' refusal of her and his preference for another, and so she hated Manolis more. Furthermore she was constantly in fear, seeing that even as a fugitive, Patouchas dared come down to the village and often slept in the homes of relatives.

Likewise, the widow's suffering continued, increasing from day to day. Manolis' absence threw her into a melancholy state, and she, who was normally so voluble, remained silent for days at a time. Only sighs would come from her chest. Then her melancholy would be succeeded by nervous irritability, unreasonable anger, tears, memories of her dear departed husband, childish airs, frequent visits to the small mirror in front of which Marghi made herself up, and, sometimes, inexplicable laughter.

Almost three months passed by and the time of the Pre-Lenten Festival came. When Zervoudhena learned that Manolis was no longer a fugitive and that his arrval was expected any day, she was so overcome with impatience that she could not find a moment's peace. She would sit down, get up, look out the window, run to the door. Whenever she heard a man's footsteps or a voice resembling Manolis', she would go outside, come back and after a few moments would run outside again. But she did not dare ask. She would only pass by Manolis' coffee-shop, which was now operated by Astronomos, and look secretly inside. That day, Nicolakis must have seen her pass by more than ten times, and he said:

"Hey, Gadfly is acting like the oxfly is goading her. What the devil's she got? She always had a loose screw, but now I see she's completely off her nut."

Marghi was overcome by anxieties of another kind. Now, finally, that Patouchas would be free, she would not only not dare go out of doors, neither would she be safe at home. With the idea that, for her, remaining any longer in the village was out of the question, she decided to go to the city once again and to remain there permanently. When the widow heard her decision:

"Do whatever you want," she said. "What can I tell you? What can I tell you?"

"And tonight I'm going to stay at my aunt's in Petrouni."

"Do whatever you want and stop bothering me," said the widow, with surprising alacrity. "Oh, go to the devil . . .!"

Next, as though regretting her unfair outburst, she sighed and seemed ready to cry.

After a while the children playing in the street in the afternoon, started shouting: "Patouchas, Patouchas." And the widow, jumping up, ran to the door and with emotion which made her tremble bodily, saw Manolis coming. He was dirty and changed, but more manly. His hair was very long and its unruliness gave him the shape of something monstrous. In order not to be totally uncovered, he had tied a black kerchief around his head, from which a tuft of hair, rising like the crest of a wild man, escaped upward. Pimples framed his sunburnt visage and his upper lip was darkened by a thickening moustache. But to the widow he seemed even more handsome than before, because he was more manly and the thickness of the moustache intensified the impression of robustness, which chiefly aroused and allured her.

"How's Marouli? shouted Manolis when he saw her. "Where is she?"

Marouli had already departed for her aunt's house.

"And what does she say?" repeated Manolis. "Does she still not want me?"

"The same. She drowns, she kills herself, she doesn't want you."

"Whether she wants to or not, I'm going to marry her, I'm going to abduct her this very night, I daresay."

The widow suddenly made a decisive gesture and said:

"Abduct her . . . What can I say?" And her lips trembled.

"Is she coming tonight or is she going to stay away at Petrouni?"

"No, she'll come," said the widow after a moment's hesitation."

Manolis proceeded to the village singing softly:

If I let this year pass me by without a mate.
I'll lose my wits and the devil with my ancestor's fate.

160

From everywhere greetings were directed to him from men and women; "Welcome, Manolio!" Some of the children who saw him ran ahead to give the good news to his mother. But Manolis, instead of going to his home or to another belonging to kinfolk, appeared in Aghia Aekaterini's square where the young people were playing "river," while the children furiously and incessantly struck a wooden gong hanging from the trunk of an aged bitter orange tree. The "river" was going around the church, when suddenly Manolis' shout was heard:

"Only brave men fight for Sfakia!"

And charging, he leapfrogged over all of the players one after the other. Then he bent over and, propping his hands on his knees, placed himself at the end of the line. There, turning his head without rising, he shouted to his peers and friends.

"How are you, my good friends? Are you okay?"

In the excitement of the game, he proposed to the youths that they all go through the village with the "river." His proposal was accepted and the "river" followed the uneven and ascending roads of the village. Gradually, others joined and the line of the "river" became quite long.

It had started getting dark when they arrived at the edge of the village, where Zervoudhena's home was. Patouchas was leaping over his fellow players two at a time with shouts of enthusiasm. But Marghi had not yet returned from Petrouni. Only the widow appeared and found a way to exchange a few whispered words with Manolis.

Saitonicolina had come out in search of him, and after a little, met him in the road; but it was in vain that she tried to take him home where the entire family was going to gather. Manolis dined at Astronomos' place. Later, getting the key to his home so he could sleep there at night, he went out, found various friends and they started going from house to house. Everywhere they found sumptuous tables, songs and dances. Manolis and his friends drank until they could drink no more. Some of them had improvised disguises. One of them, for instance, had passed his feet through the sleeves of his overcoat, so he would look like he was wearing European attire, and pretended he was a doctor. Another had fashioned a turban around his head; a third had put on a dress pretending he was Deli Marian, a half-crazy local woman. Manolis also tried to imitiate the garb of a doctor and to wear tight fitting clothes, but all he managed to do was tear the sleeves off a coat. How could those big feet get through? Therefore, abandoning the ambition to disguise himself as a European, he started acting like a billy-goat. And he entered the houses on all fours, bleating. The men burst out laughing, while the women, among whom he rushed by preference, retreated uneasily before the manlike beast with four feet and laughed as though tickled when the Satyr approached.

It was almost midnight when he left his friends. The village was already asleep and silence prevailed, interrupted from time to time only by sounds of the cocks. Manolis, drunk and tottering, directed himself towards his home. But on the way a sudden recollection stopped him. "Where are you going, my good fellow?" he murmured addressing himself. "Where are you going, my good fellow?" He stopped and thought for a few moments, then he turned back. And as he advanced staggering he mumbled:

"Do you think it's up to you to decide . . .? Want it or not . . .you're just being pigheaded, isn't that so? Then I'm abducting you. I'm taking you by force. Who do you think I am . . .? I stood up to the Albanians and the Moudir . . . I'm not afraid of anyone . . . You're just being pigheaded. Today your pigheadedness ends."

Speaking to himself in this manner he reached Zervoudhena's home, which was completely shut up and completely dark, like all those of its neighbors, like all those of the village. Manolis stopped and appeared pensive, but it is certain that he was not thinking about anything. Rather he was sleeping on two feet. Then he neared the gateway and, with some difficulty, went up the few steps of the outer door. He stood still for a few moments, then he pulled out a dagger and directed its point between the doorframe and the door and began to try to pull back the wooden latch. His efforts continued for some time, not because of the difficulty of the undertaking so much as by his drunken clumsiness. The latch had started to pull back, when the dagger escaped from his hand and fell noisily. Manolis, even as inebriated as he was, was frightened. He remained still for a few seconds and listened. But within the house calm and silence prevailed. Then, bending to pick up his dagger, he almost fell and rolled under the porch. Supporting himself, he got hold of the knife and continued his efforts which would soon succeed. The latch moved all the way back, and the door too yielded to a soft push with only a little sigh of the hinges.

Manolis bent down at the partially opened door but did not hear any sound. The widow and her daughter had not awakened.Inside the house it was pitch dark, but Manolis knew the high sofa on which the girl slept and went to it, trying not to make any noise. He found the short ladder leading up to the divan by feeling his way about and went up two or three steps. He stopped again. From the bed before him he could hear her breathing. Manolis groped about with his outstreched hand; then encircling her with his arms, lifted her covers and all to his arms, climbed down the steps of the sofa and turned towards the door. A few moments later he was in the street, and off he went with his load at the greatest speed his complaining feet would permit. Drunk as he was, he was impressed by the paradox that the abducted girl neither cried out nor tried to resist, nor did she even move or jerk. But he was drunk enough for his thought not to go beyond this observation. His route in that darkness where he had to fumble his way around was so bumpy that it rather disturbed and dulled his mind. The only thing that was clear in the fog of his brain was the need for haste. And he moved as quickly as he could, running the danger of stumbling and falling down along with his burden.

He arrived at his house and his abducted prey remained motionless. Then, Manolis, while busy opening the door of his shop, was able to find explanation to this strange immobility. He assumed that Marouli, seeing the futility of resistance, had submitted to superior force.

Entering the shop, he placed his load on a wooden bench and lit the lamp. But when he turned with the light he was astounded and a great portion of his drunkenness was dissolved at once. Instead of the daughter, he had in front of him the mother. The widow was dressed and it seemed that she had not slept. Trembling bodily, she stood there looking down as if she was a prisoner.

Manolis stepped back a little and stared at her with wide-open eyes, as if he were seeing a ghost, and he said in a choking voice:

"It's you! You? To the devil with your ancestors."

The widow lifted her crazed eyes toward him and, in an imploring, tearful voice, said to him:

"Don't you like me, Manolio?"

This was the great, the enormous admission which for so long had oppressed her breast without her being able to utter it. Manolis shuddered. That phrase completely illuminated his incomprehending brain. Finally, he understood the widow's odd behavior of late and the garbled words which she spoke to him.

"And where's Marouli?" he said to her.

"How do I know? How do I know?" the widow answered in a distracted manner. "She stayed over with her aunt at Petrouni. Why do you want her since she doesn't want you, and she says she's going to the city again? What do you want her for?"

And approaching the young man with the meek supplicating manner of a dog, she repeated:

"Don't you like me, Manolio?"

Her voice was broken off by a fit of sobs.

"Don't you like me . . .? Me, who's loved you for such a long time, poor unfortunate me?"

Manolis was looking her over from head to foot as if her words had begun to tempt him. Then a wave of wrath rose on his face and flashed in his eyes.

"Out! Out!" he shouted with a terrible voice. "Go to the devil and don't let anybody see you, you crazy woman!"

The widow raised her imploring eyes filling with tears to him, while her lips trembled.

Don't you feel sorry for me?" she pleaded.

In answer Patouchas raised his terrible foot, ready to expel her with a kick:

"Go away I tell you! The devil take your ancestors, before I kill you!"

The widow, having looked at him with a prolonged glance in which a last hope trembled, sighed and the sigh arose from her breast as a wail. Then she went to the door and went out.

Manolis could hear her for a few moments as she went away wailing in the darkness.

"Lord, what humiliation! Lord, what a humiliation," he said, holding his forehead.

His drunkenness had almost completely evaporated. He went to the doorway, and sitting on the bench, set his head on his hand and stayed there thinking. The night was chilly, but Manolis did not feel the cold. Dawn found him still there. During this time, he sighed frequently and it seems that his craziness was dissipating with those sighs and leaving him to consider the situation coolly. But what exactly went on in that crazy head, we cannot know. Only this is known, that at noon, while Saitonicolis was eating, he saw the rebel coming, humble and reserved.

"Did you get over it?" he said to him smiling. "I knew what I was saying."

"Forgive me, father," Manolis said with an air of a saint, and bending kissed the paternal hand. "I'll marry whoever you want."

"You know who I want. They call her Pighi. Come, sit down . . . And so your craziness doesn't overcome you again, for better or for worse, we'll get you engaged at once, tonight, and get you married at Easter.

And, indeed, in the evening Saitonicolis, accompanied by Manolis, his wife and other relatives, went to Thomas'. A radiant Pighi welcomed them and, approaching Manolis, she whispered to him:

"Are our troubles over, Manolio?"

Manolis blushed and felt the enchantment of those eyes master him again. That evening the round fez appeared to him as tame as a night cap, and at the table he clinked his glass with Stratis, who wished him well:

"To a happy marriage, brother-in-law."

After a while a female relative came and announced that the widow, Zervoudhena, had gone mad and all day long she repeated a single prhase: "Why don't you like me?"

"That poor woman!" Saitonicolis said. "But she was a little touched from the start."

Manolis was disturbed, partly because he felt sorry, and because he felt that he had contributed to her misfortune, and partly from fear. But his fear was quieted by the darkness of the night and the darkness of her madness which had securely covered up his final act of craziness and his shame.

The wedding took place the Sunday following Easter. Two or three days later, Manolis met Tereres and when he saw him at a distance, he raised his arm in a gesture of defiance and, laughing boisterously, shouted to him:

"Here's to you and your magic!"

FOOTNOTES

[1] Andonis Decavalles, "The Development of Modern Greek Prose," *The Charioteer* No. 5 (1963), p. 80.

[2] Alkis Thrylos, "Hellenes Degematographi: Ioannis Kondylakis," (Greek Prose Writers: Ioannis Kondylakis), NEA HESTIA, XII (Nov., 1932) p. 1169.

[3] André M. Andréadès, "Trois étapes de la littérature grecque moderne, *"Oeuvres* Vol. III *Miscellanées.* Edited by K. Ch. Varvaressos; G.A. Petropoulos and J.D. Pintos. Athènes: Faculté de droit de l'Université d'Athènes, 1940, p. 123.

[4] Falanga: a form of punishment or, if carried to extremes, torture in which the feet are beaten.

[5] In 826, Crete was conquered by Saracens from Spain. They were driven out in 961 by the Byzantines. Here Saracen means any Arab.

[6] Hanoum: the categorical name of any one of the many wives of a Turkish nobleman.

[7] Rayah: a Greek Christian subject of the Turkish Empire.

[8] Palikari: A member of the band of a Greek or Albanian military chief especially during the war of Independence. In modern usage it has come to mean a young man with all the good qualities of youth.

[9] Hookah: Water-pipe.

[10] Agha: Turkish for an officer of high military or civil rank.

[11] Bey: Turkish for the governor of a minor Turkish province or district.

[12] Raki: An anise-flavored alcoholic beverage.

[13] Luckmann: An Arab who wrote a collection of myths and maxims.

[14] Ell: An ancient measure of length originally represented by the length of the forearm; about 18-20 inches.

[15] Oke: 2.83 pounds equals one oke.

[16] This and other similar sayings expressed the wish of all the Greeks for the liberation of this "Greek" city.

[17] Barba: Respectful term of address to older people.

[18] Mer-haba: Turkish greeting.

[19] Koubare: Means both godfather and best-man. It is often used as a friendly term of address. Koubara is the feminine form of the same term.

[20] Mizithra: A mild, soft, moist Greek cheese made from the the whey drained from feta, mixed with ewe's milk.

[21] Bourmas: A Cretan of Christian origin who has become a Moslem.

[22] Misirlides: People from Misiri in Egypt.

[23] Traditionally god-parents had the right to name a child.

[24] Achladia: Pear tree.

[25] Achladhi: Female name deriving directly from the Greek word for pear tree.

[26] Melia: Apple tree.

[27] Triantaphylia: Rose bush.

[28] "May the devil take your ancestors" has a deeper meaning than "go to the devil," as it might have been otherwise be translated, because of the importance of ancestors in family tradition.

[29] Franks: From the time of the Crusades, the Greeks called all Western Europeans Franks.

[30] Mandrake: A person reputed to be practising magic.

[31] Kastro: In Byzantine and Frankish Greece many large fortified metropolitan areas were called "Kastro" from the Latin *castra* (military camp).

[32] Mode: One of several patterned arrangements characteristic of Classical Greek and Byzantine Church music.

[33] A saying bearing the wish that Manolis will also be the best man at his godchild's wedding.

[34] Presbytera: The title of the wife of a Greek Orthodox priest.

[35] Consuls: Diplomatic representatives of the Western European powers who mediated the affairs of Crete until Crete's reunion with Greece in 1912.

[36] Hati-houmayoun: A Turkish decree passed on in 1856, by which a number of Greeks were set free after the Turkish defeat during the Crimean War.

[37] Rials: Turkish money

[38] Epitaphios: Refers to the Orthodox custom of decorating an epitaphion (sepulcher of Christ) for the Good Friday services.

[39] Adio: A sophisticated way of saying goodbye. Here it shows Marghi's influence from the city. It is a foreign word picked up during the Frankish occupation.

[40] Equivalent to: You can't make a silk purse out of a sow's ear.

[41] A female Moslem name.

[42] Does a teetotaller know what beer is?

[43] Danaids: In Greek mythology, the fifty daughters of Danaus who, with the exception of Hypermnestra, murdered their husbands, the sons of Hegyptus, on their bridal night at their father's command.

[44] Digenis: A Greek legendary figure known for his valour and about whose feats many folk songs have been written.

[45] Kariofili: Greek name for rifles, originating from the rifles made by the Italian firm, Carlo e Figli.

[46] Casting a spell by means of which Manolis would become sexually impotent.

[47] An upland plain in Central Crete.

[48] An insulting gesture.

[49] In Greece, people usually dress in black when a relative dies.

[50] A Greek expression which means, "I'll show you who's the boss."

[51] Mattinada: Often improvised couplet of romantic or humorous content sung to a striking melody.

[52] Dolmades: Greek dish prepared by stuffing vine leaves with ground beef and spices.

[53] He loves me, he loves me not.

[54] Spinning: Twisting cotton into thread by using a distaff.

[55] Mi sasirma oghloum: "Don't get confused, my son, and follow the path of the infidel."

[56] An insulting gesture.

[57] *Erotokritos:* (ca 1645), a masterpiece of Cretan literature, by Vitzentzos Kornaros. Based on *Paris et Vienne,* its plot is adapted to the Cretan character and ideals. It has as its theme the chivalrous love of the hero, Erotokritos, for the princess, Arethousa, daughter of King Heracles of Athens.

[58] Rend her clothes: An exaggerated expression of distress while making a plea to a higher authority.

[59] Lyra: A Cretan musical string instrument resembling a violin.

[60] Pidhiktos: A Cretan dance characterized by jumping.

[61] Sighanos: Cretan dance characterized by slow movements.

[62] Janissaries, men of Greek blood taken from their parents' homes as children and raised as Turkish soldiers.

[63] Pre-Lenten Festival: This period used to consist of feasting and costume partying. It is like the European Carnival Season.